TIME STO**!**

TERROR
IN HAWK'S
VILLAGE

Written by
Karla Warkentin

Illustrated by
Ron Adair

COLLECT THEM ALL!
Rescue in the Mayan Jungle
Mystery in the Medieval Castle
Treachery in the Ancient Laboratory
Terror in Hawk's Village

Equipping Kids for Life

An Imprint of Cook Communications Ministries
Colorado Springs, CO

Faith
Building
Guide
Ages
9 and up
Remembering

A Faith Building Guide can
be found on page 131.

Faith Kidz® is an imprint of Cook Communications Ministries
Colorado Springs, Colorado 80918
Cook Communications, Paris, Ontario
Kingsway Communications, Eastbourne, England

TERROR IN HAWK'S VILLAGE
©2004 by Karla Marie Krahn-Warkentin

First printing, 2004
Printed in the United States
1 2 3 4 5 6 7 8 9 10 Printing/Year 08 07 06 05 04

Editor: Heather Gemmen
Design Manager: Nancy L. Haskins
Cover Designer: Image Studios
Cover Illustrator: Ron Adair
Interior Designer: Pat Miller
ISBN: 0781440262

Dedicated with love to
Ingrid Friesen and Cindy Klassen.
Thank you for your friendship,
encouragement, and prayers.
Our Thursday afternoons are priceless.

I am grateful for the contributions of my husband, Randy;
Dr. Gus Konkel; Ron Adair; Carol Ann Hiemstra;
Heather Gemmen; Wayne and Phyllis Banman; Rachel Dyck;
Ingrid Friesen; Linda Janzen; Cindy Klassen; Marie Peters;
Mary Poetker; Sharon Toews; Grace Warkentin;
and everyone at
Cook Communications Ministries.
Each one of you has left an indelible mark on this series.

A special thank you to my remarkable friend, Elaine MacNeish,
who willingly shared her time, knowledge, and heart for the Lord.

"Remember the Sabbath day by keeping it holy.
Six days shall you labor and do all your work,
but the seventh day is a Sabbath to the LORD your God.
On it you shall not do any work,
neither you, nor your son or daughter,
nor your manservant or maidservant,
nor your animals, nor the alien within your gates.
For in six days the LORD made the heavens and the earth,
the sea, and all that is in them,
but he rested on the seventh day.
Therefore the LORD blessed the Sabbath day
and made it holy."
Exodus 20:8-11

Contents

1   Leaving   7

2   Vision Quest   11

3   The Perfect Day   23

4   Hawk's Village   35

5   Attack   47

6   Miracles   59

7   The Council Fire   73

8   The Delegation   89

9   Betrayed   97

10   Battle of the Canoes   109

11   Deadfalls and Snares   115

12   The Feast   123

Faith Building Guide   131

— ONE —

LEAVING

I hate weeding," declared Josh, crouching over a row of peas. He brushed his long, blond bangs out of his eyes for the hundredth time that hour. "It's the worst possible job in the world—a total waste of a Saturday night."

"I agree," said Ellen, grabbing a huge thistle Josh had missed. She gave it a firm tug. It came out in one piece, roots and all, and she shoved it in his face. "How could you miss this one? It's obviously a weed." Ellen was fifteen years old and had just had another growth spurt, ending up two heads taller than her eleven-year-old twin brothers and almost as tall as her dad. "The only reason we're out here is because you didn't want to weed the garden earlier. You were too busy skateboarding."

"She's right. It's all your fault, Josh. You know I like to get my chores over with in the morning," added his brother, Will. Even though they were twins and got along most of the time, he made a point of blaming his brother for everything possible.

Josh stood up, wiped the sweat off his brow, tucked his bangs behind one ear, and stretched. "You're lucky we're doing this now. It was a lot hotter this afternoon. The thermometer on the side of the garage said 35°C. Besides, we're only two days into our summer holidays. It doesn't matter when we do our chores. We've got two long months to get them done."

"Oh, no, we don't," said Ellen. "Mom said we had to get the weeding done today, or else she'd give us three extra jobs."

Josh scowled. "What's the big hurry?"

"Twenty ladies from church are coming over for lunch tomorrow."

"If we get extra jobs, you get mine," said Will. He looked down and inspected his freshly pressed khaki shorts and the front of his white polo shirt. There was one tiny speck of dirt on his chest. He carefully flicked it back onto the ground.

"That's not fair," said Josh, dropping his work gloves to the ground. "Why should I have to do all *your* work?"

"Because if we don't finish this tonight, it's all your fault. If it were up to me, we'd have done our work first thing this morning, before it got hot, and I'd be sitting in my room with a cold glass of lemonade right now, reading."

"Okay, okay. I get the picture." Josh struck his teapot pose; he placed one hand on his hip and dangled the other hand in the air, like the little teapot in the nursery rhyme. "Hi, I'm just Super-Will," he said in a high-pitched voice, "and I just love to sit around in my fancy clothes and read. Read, read, read, that's all I do, and oh, I'm just so, so, so smart. Just call me Will, the smart boy."

Will stuck out his tongue. Ellen turned away, trying not to laugh. Since Josh didn't get the reaction he'd hoped for, he plopped down on the dirt and pulled a round, fist-sized stone out of his pocket. He turned it over and studied the symbols on it carefully, lost in thought. The three of them called it the "time stone."

The time stone had appeared on their front yard several months ago. It looked like a regular stone, except that its top and bottom were a bit flat, and it had strange symbols carved across it. Every once in a while, a tiny hole appeared in the side of the stone, and it projected a series of pictures onto the nearest wall. If somebody touched the stone while it was projecting, a whirlwind appeared and mysteriously transported them back in time to the scene that was being displayed. So far, they had visited a Mayan jungle, a medieval castle, and an ancient laboratory. During each trip, they helped the people they met solve some difficult problems and learned something new about God. Josh still didn't know what triggered the stone to project these images. It seemed to come alive on its own. After each trip, one of the symbols on the stone vanished, its grooves filled in so perfectly that you'd never guess a symbol had been there before.

Will glanced at his brother. When he noticed the stone in Josh's hand, he turned as white as a sheet. "Why did you bring the stone out here? You promised you'd keep it in your drawer for a while. I need a break. I'm not ready to go on another trip."

The first two trips had been terrifying, particularly for Will. While Josh loved adventure and seemed to thrive in unpredictable situations, Will needed order and safety. Ellen's approach was more philosophical. She could analyze the unusual circumstances they found themselves in, without letting fear or worry overcome her.

Josh lovingly ran his fingers over the remaining seven symbols. "I sure wish I knew what these mean. I bet they're important."

"What's important is that you put that thing away before it transports us again. I almost got killed on our first two trips. The trip to the laboratory was the only one that was any good."

"Oh, come on, you liked being a knight. I could tell," teased Ellen.

"I did not. I like staying at home. This is where I belong," he said pointing to the ground. "Everything is safe here, just the way I like it."

Just then Josh heard a little clicking noise. A hole opened in the side of the time stone, and even though it was light outside, a hologram of a village floated in the air in front of them. "Look!" he shouted.

A cluster of wigwams, nestled in the forest, hung in the air. A group of dark-skinned warriors was sitting in a circle around a fire, talking. Machetes, tomahawks, and spears lay scattered on the ground around them. The head warrior wore a feathered headdress, and he had a stern look on his face as he spoke, gesturing with his hand toward the woods.

Will gasped. "Don't move. We're not going there. Look at those weapons. They could easily kill us." He took a step toward Josh.

"Will, relax. Nothing has happened yet," said Ellen.

"You call a hologram *nothing?*"

"I didn't know the stone could work outside. This is great," exclaimed Josh. Without realizing what he was doing, he tightened his fingers around it. Immediately everything around them fell silent; even the crickets stopped chirping. As they stood there, Josh held his breath and stared wide-eyed at Will and Ellen as he waited for something to happen.

A smile stole onto his face when a loud whoosh of air rushed through the yard. His smile vanished when the ground started rippling in great waves beneath them. The waves picked up speed; they came faster and faster. It took all of his strength and coordination to keep from falling.

Will grabbed Ellen and let out a piercing scream. He didn't stop until a tornado-like whirlwind dropped out of the sky, landing on top of them. Everything went black when it sucked them up and carried them away.

VISION QUEST

CXBNEXXXBNEXXXBNEXXXBNEXXBO

J osh opened his eyes. The sunlight was blinding, so he quickly scrunched them shut. He rolled to his left, shielded his face with his hand, and cautiously opened his eyes again. A steep rock face loomed above him.

"Guys, don't roll back. If you do, you'll fall into the lake," barked Will. The three of them sat up and quickly slid backward on the ledge until their backs were resting against the rock face. "Why did we have to land here? I'm a lousy swimmer."

"Where are we?" asked Josh, ignoring Will's grumbling.

"I don't know, but it sure is beautiful," said Ellen. Miles of rugged shoreline spread out around them, bordered by a forest of birch, cedar, and poplar trees. Giant pines dotted the rocky cliffs, towering over the rest of the forest. It was amazing how they could thrive with only bare rock to anchor their roots.

All was quiet except for the gentle rustling of the breeze. Even the lake was as still as a sheet of glass. A little ways down the shore, a white-tailed deer and her fawn cautiously crept up to the water's edge and took a drink before disappearing back into the forest. Josh took a deep breath. A sense of peace came over him, a welcome calm after their whirlwind journey. He could feel his body relax as he sat there. A little way out, a fish jumped, breaking the mirror-like surface of the water.

"I'm definitely not going swimming," muttered Will.

"Do whatever you want," he said, not letting Will ruin the new-found calm that had settled in his heart. He crawled to the edge of the rock, looked down, and then spun around, motioning for Will and Ellen to join him.

They crawled over to Josh and lay down on their stomachs beside him. Down below, a blue heron stood absolutely still on toothpick-thin legs, its long, pointy beak hovering over the water. As they watched, it jabbed its head underwater and came up with a small fish dangling from its bill. Suddenly it tipped its head back, swallowed the fish whole, spread its great wings, and slowly flew away.

"What a beautiful bird," sighed Ellen.

"Great, just what I need, wildlife central," grumbled Will.

"Are you planning on being a grouch all day? If you are, you can stay here while Josh and I explore."

"Quit bossing me around. You're not my mother," Will replied, scowling.

Ellen stood up. "I know I'm not your mother, but I can choose who I spend my time with. Just because you're my brother doesn't mean you automatically qualify. Lighten up!" She turned toward the rock face and gasped. "Guys, get up! Look!"

The cliff behind them was covered in red drawings. Moose, birds, stick people, and handprints abounded, interspersed by the occasional wigwam and canoe.

Will's eyes darted back and forth. "Somebody's been here before. What if they're watching us?"

Josh and Ellen were too busy huddling over a particularly strange group of paintings to listen to what he was saying. The first drawing showed one person standing over another person lying on the ground. Squiggly lines joined their heads together. The next picture showed a person joined by a squiggly line to a flying bird. In the last one, two people stood side by side. A squiggly line joined the mouth of the smaller person to a hole in the chest of the larger one.

"What's with those lines?" asked Josh.

"Maybe it means they're talking," said Ellen.

Will looked at them, wide-eyed. "Maybe it means they're using ESP."

Josh scrunched up his nose. "What's that?"

"Extrasensory perception. It means you can talk to someone without actually speaking, by using the power of your mind." Will's eyes opened even wider. "What if they're watching us, reading our minds right now?" He scanned their surroundings, but all he could see were rocks, trees, and water. "I don't see anyone, but think nice thoughts just in case."

"That's creepy. I hope you're wrong," said Ellen.

"Me, too."

They moved over to the next drawing. A person with a halo over his head juggled a variety of sticks and small dogs.

Will gulped. "What if they can read our minds while they juggle dogs? What if they're giants?"

"Do you have any idea how ridiculous you sound? You're letting your imagination get away from you. Just because there's a picture of someone juggling dogs doesn't mean they're a giant. Remember when we landed in Golden Lane? When Josh saw those small houses he thought the people were leprechauns. That wasn't true at all. There's no point in getting all worked up until we have some concrete facts," said Ellen.

As his sister droned on, a funny feeling ran down Josh's spine, that sense you get when you know someone is watching you. He looked over his shoulder; there was a wide span of water and a few seagulls. He turned to his left and then his right, but all he could see was rocky shoreline and acres of untamed forest. Feeling like he was still missing something, he slowly looked up and gasped.

"What?" said Ellen.

"Look up," he whispered.

A boy was perched on the ridge above them. It was hard to discern his age. He appeared to be the same size as the twins, yet he looked older somehow. He was bare-chested and bare-legged—all he wore was a buckskin breechcloth—so Josh couldn't help but notice his muscular build and the long scar that ran down his right arm. The boy's glossy black hair hung down his back in two thick braids. A square pouch decorated with a blue-and-green diamond pattern was tied around his waist. He placed his hand on it as he examined the three of them with dark, serious eyes, and then he lifted his bow and arrow and aimed it directly at them.

Josh thrust his hands above his head. "Don't shoot!"

The boy flinched and stared at them some more.

"He doesn't understand. What do we do now?" said Ellen, her voice quaking.

"I don't know," whispered Josh.

"I knew we shouldn't have come here. What if he shoots us?" moaned Will. His eyes rolled back until only the whites were showing, and he started to wobble back and forth.

"No, don't faint, not now," groaned Josh. He and Ellen grabbed Will and propped him up so he wouldn't keel over.

Much to their surprise, the boy slowly lowered his bow and arrow and laid them on the ground. He looked up at the sky and whispered what appeared to be a prayer as a bald eagle flew overhead. Josh gave the boy a fleeting glance—he was still praying—and watched the eagle as it soared across the sky on its enormous wings. When it was almost out of sight, the boy backed away from the ridge and disappeared into the woods.

Will pulled away from Josh and Ellen, blinking rapidly as he came to his senses. "Good, I'm glad he's gone. That bow and arrow made me nervous. Let's find the stone and get out of here."

Ellen put her hands on her hips and glowered at him. "Hello, earth calling Will. Where have you been the last three trips? You know the stone doesn't reappear until it's time for us to go home. We need to find out why we've been sent here and get on with it."

"I'm passing on this one. We have no idea where we are, and that guy looked really dangerous. This already reminds me of our trip to the jungle, and we all know how bad that one was. I'm not interested in being captured by a tribe of warriors out here in the middle of nowhere. As far as I'm concerned, the journey is over. I'm finding a way home."

"But it doesn't work like that, and you know it. Quit being such a big chicken."

"I can be a chicken if I want. Go on without me. I'll be fine."

"Um, guys," interrupted Josh, "take a look at three o'clock."

Will and Ellen turned to the right. The boy was walking across the rocky ledge toward them. "Boo-zhoo," he said, nodding, and then he repeated himself. "Boo-zhoo."

"He's calling you a 'bozo' with a funny accent, Josh. We need to get out of here," hissed Will.

Josh whacked him on the arm. "Be quiet. He's just saying hello."

"What?"

"Boo-zhoo means 'hello' in his language. Be quiet so I can concentrate."

"You mean you can understand him and I can't?" sulked Will.

"If you'd quit thinking about yourself for once, maybe you'd under-stand him, too." Josh slowly walked over to the boy. He let his arms hang loosely at his sides and plastered a cheerful smile onto his face, trying to appear as nonthreatening as possible. "Hi, I'm Josh. We're here to visit you."

"Are you Nanabozho?" asked the boy.

"Who?"

"I've never heard of Nanabozho before," whispered Ellen.

The boy frowned. "You are as pale as the owl. Are you the paleface the elders have dreamed of from the great faraway?"

Josh shrugged. "I don't know. I suppose we might look kind of pale to you, and we did come from a long way away."

"What's he saying?" said Will. "I've never heard that language before. How come you can understand him and I can't?"

Ellen turned to her brother. "I don't know why we can understand him, but this is the way it's been on all the trips. Maybe it has something to do with you."

"I understood everything in England."

"Yeah, but they were speaking English there, although it was the strangest English I'd ever heard," said Josh. "Maybe you can't understand because you have a bad attitude."

"I don't have a bad attitude," grumbled Will.

Ellen gave him a sympathetic smile. "Josh is right. Your attitude stinks."

"How am I supposed to be? We've never seen this guy before, we don't know where we are, and I don't understand anything he's saying. This feels horrible."

"Ellen and I understand him," said Josh smugly. "He asked if we're the paleface."

"Tell him we're not. I don't want to agree to that until I know whether a paleface is a good or bad thing. What if they eat them?"

"You know, Will, it's at moments like this that I'm embarrassed you're my brother. We need to concentrate on him, not you. If you can't understand, be quiet and let us do the talking," said Ellen.

"Good idea," agreed Josh.

Ellen turned her attention back to the boy. "Sorry about that. What are you doing out here?"

"I just finished my vision quest. I was about to head back to my people when I heard your voices and decided to investigate," he replied.

"What's your name?" asked Josh.

"White Hawk, but my family calls me Hawk."

Josh smiled. "That's a great name; I wish I had a name like that. Who are your people?"

"I'm an Ojibwa."

"Really?"

The boy nodded.

"By the way, I'm Josh, and this is my sister, Ellen, and that's my brother, Will." He put his hand into his pocket and pulled out a half-eaten granola bar. "Oh, good. I was getting hungry." He peeled back the foil wrapper, inspected the lint that was coating the open end, and took a bite. "Tho, wazz a vizin kezt?" Little crumbs spilled out the sides of his mouth.

Ellen grabbed him by the arm. "Don't talk with your mouth full."

Hawk reached over, took the granola bar from Josh's hand, sniffed it, and popped it—wrapper and all—into his mouth. Josh gave Ellen a perturbed look, but she was too busy watching Hawk to notice. He immediately pulled the wrapper out of his mouth and examined it. Then he spit the granola bar onto the ground and stood there, his tongue hanging out of his mouth, as he rubbed it against his top teeth, trying to scrape off the remaining bits of Josh's snack.

Not satisfied with his effort, he turned and ran into the woods. Josh and Ellen followed him and watched him wipe his tongue on the leaves of a tree.

"I like that," whispered Josh. "He's my kind of guy."

"That does look like something you would do," she agreed.

His tongue now clean, Hawk scrambled down the rocks to the water's edge. Josh and Ellen joined Will back on the ridge and watched as Hawk used his hands to take a drink. As they stood there, Will closed his eyes and took one deep breath after another.

"What are you doing?" asked Josh.

He shook his hand at them. "Be quiet. I'm doing breathing exercises so I can relax."

Josh scrunched up his face. "Why do you need to relax?"

"So I can understand that guy's language."

Josh looked at Ellen, twirled his finger at the side of his head, pointed at Will, and mouthed the word, "Cuckoo."

She nodded in agreement.

Hawk climbed back up to Josh and Ellen and continued their conversation as if nothing had happened.

"When we are old enough to leave our childish ways behind, the people of my tribe go into the woods by themselves for their vision quest. We fast and pray until we have visions and meet our guardian manitou." Will's face lit up with a big smile. He punched his fist into the air. "I can understand him. Yes!" When he realized what he had done, he turned red and quickly pulled his hand down to his side. "Oh, sorry. I didn't mean to do that."

Hawk continued on. "Our guardian manitous teach us what path we are to take for our lives. My vision helped me answer some of my biggest questions, like how I think about my creator and the path I need to take in my life so that I can use the skills he has given me."

"That sounds serious," said Josh.

"What's a manitou?" asked Ellen.

"It's our dream spirit that stays with us wherever we go. It gives us power when we need it and teaches us how to live a good life."

Josh frowned. "I've never heard of that before. What do these manitou things look like?"

"They usually look like animals, often bears, moose, or eagles. Mine was different, though."

"What was yours?"

Hawk looked away; he wouldn't say a word.

"Whatever," muttered Josh. He looked at Ellen. "I guess he doesn't want to talk about it."

"Are you going back to your village now?" asked Ellen.

"Yes. We always fast during our vision quests. I haven't eaten in ten days. I can hardly wait to see my mother. She promised to have some rabbit stew ready for me when I return."

Ellen grimaced.

"It's okay. It probably tastes like chicken," said Josh.

"Considering that comment came from a guy who's always hungry and eats anything, I don't necessarily believe you."

Josh flashed her a smile. "Hey, Hawk, do you think we could come with you to your village?"

Will jumped up from his spot on a nearby rock and started flapping his hands in the air. "Wait! Just a minute! We need to talk about this first. You can't just go and volunteer to follow this guy to his village. We don't know anything about him. What if his people want to hurt us? I think we should stay here."

"No way. If it was up to you, we'd just sit on this ledge for days and watch the sun go up and down. That would be boring," scoffed Josh.

"Come on, Will, you know how this works. Can't you cooperate for once without making a fuss?" begged Ellen.

Will shook his head. "We have no idea what we're getting into. For all we know, they might kill us on sight."

"I'm positive God won't let that happen. You can stay if you want. I'm going with Josh and Hawk," she said. "Come on, guys. Let's go."

Ellen and Josh followed Hawk off the ledge, but Will didn't budge. He stood there, his feet firmly planted on the ground, with a determined look on his face. They walked a little way down the shoreline until they reached a narrow sand beach. A small birch-bark canoe had been pulled up onto the sand. Although it was a little banged up, it was obvious that skill had gone into its construction. Long sheets of bark covered the thin cedar frame. They were sewn on with roots from pine trees, and the entire canoe was sealed with a mixture of pitch. Hawk grabbed his paddle, and Josh and Ellen helped him push the canoe into the water. The two of them climbed into the front, and then Hawk gave the canoe a big push and jumped into the back. He dipped his paddle into the water, and they were off.

About ten seconds later, Will came tearing down the beach, yelling at the top of his lungs. "Wait for me! I was just joking! I want to come, too!"

Hawk stopped paddling and looked at Josh and Ellen.

"We can't just leave him there. He'd never survive on his own," said Ellen.

"It would serve him right. Why does he always have to be so difficult?" muttered Josh.

"That's just how he is. I thought he'd be getting better at this adventure stuff by now."

The current continued to pull them away from shore. Will became even more animated, jumping up and down and waving his arms. "Don't leave me! I want to come, too!"

Ellen let out a big sigh. "Hawk, do you mind going back?"

He shook his head.

"Sorry. Will can be a bit difficult."

Hawk turned the canoe around and paddled back to shore. Will sloshed through the water until he was knee-deep. When the canoe was within reach, he threw himself in, landing on top of his brother and sister.

"Once you were gone, I realized I didn't want to stay by myself," he said breathlessly.

"Next time do you think you could figure that out sooner?" suggested Josh.

Will stuck out his tongue.

Hawk's long smooth strokes steadily propelled the canoe across the calm waters of the lake. The quiet was almost unsettling. There were no motorboats, power lines, or houses—just miles and miles of pristine shoreline, untouched by civilization.

He stopped paddling as they neared a section of land at what appeared to be the end of the lake. Several small plumes of smoke rose up ahead of them. "That's my village. We stay here for the summer until our group separates and moves to the winter hunting grounds." Just past his village, the lake emptied into a wide river.

A few minutes later they reached the village's sand beach. A large assortment of birch-bark canoes was lined up against the breathtaking backdrop of the woods. Some of the canoes were tiny, only big enough for two people, and others were enormous, capable of holding twenty passengers or more. With a few more strokes, Hawk had the tip of their canoe on the shore. A scrawny-looking, brown spotted dog bounded through the woods toward them, sniffed the air, and let out a sharp yelp. Hawk leaped out of the canoe, patted the dog's head as he passed by, and skipped up a deeply beaten path through the woods.

"What about us? What are we supposed to do?" yelled Josh.

Hawk turned and held up his hand. "Wait. I'll get my stew, and then we'll go back on the lake."

"But I thought you were going to show us your village."

"First I have to take my turn scouting."

"What's that?" shouted Will.

Hawk took three steps toward them. "Watching for danger."

Will gulped. "What kind of danger are we talking about?"

"There are often warring tribes in the area. We need to stay alert. We can be on the lookout while we explore." He spun around and continued up the path.

Josh's eyes lit up. "That sounds good to me."

"Warring tribes sounds *good?*" Will stood up in the canoe. It began rocking from side to side. He quickly leaned forward, resting one hand on either side of the canoe, and half stood, half crouched, as he peered up the path over the top of his glasses. "I don't like this plan at all. I want to go home."

THREE

THE PERFECT DAY

A bout ten minutes later, Hawk glided back down the path carrying a small birch-bark bowl and a wooden spoon. He shifted both objects to one hand, gave the canoe a big push, and jumped in. As they drifted out to the open water, he gobbled down the stew, put his container down, and began to paddle away from the island.

They traveled parallel to the shore for about twenty minutes. Despite Hawk's silence, Josh felt a comforting sense of peace. The lake and woods around them were tranquil, and the steady rhythm of Hawk's paddle was comforting. Even Will was quiet, if only for the moment.

They had just passed another tall, sheer rock face when Hawk shifted his paddle to the other side of the canoe and brought them in to shore. Their prow made a quiet hiss as it landed on the sand. Josh jumped out, his feet sinking in the wet sand, and helped Hawk pull the canoe out of the water. Will and Ellen hopped out, and Hawk led them single file down a narrow path in the woods, not saying a word.

Will quickened his pace so he could walk beside his brother. "Has Hawk said anything about where we are?"

"Not to me," replied Josh.

"Me, neither," said Ellen, "but I have a feeling we're in North America. I've seen woods like these when we've been on vacation."

"Then why doesn't he speak English, and why haven't we seen any other white people?" asked Josh.

"Maybe Ellen's wrong. Maybe we're not in North America," said Will.

Josh looked even more confused. "Then where would we be?"

"I'm sure we're in North America. Look around," said Ellen, pointing at the woods around them. "There are trees and water like this within driving distance of our home. Maybe we're the first white people here."

Josh's eyes lit up. "Whoa, that would be good!"

Will stopped in the middle of the path and crossed his arms over his chest. "I'm not saying I agree with Ellen, but if she's right, the latest we could be here is the 1600s because that's when the first white people arrived. For all we know, it could be hundreds of years before that, because people like Hawk lived the same way for a long time. They weren't always trying to invent new things to make their lives better. They were happy the way they were."

Josh looked down the path. "Um, guys, where's Hawk?"

Ellen squinted as she looked for him. "He must have gone on without us."

"Oh, I don't feel good," moaned Will. "We need to find him. We'll never find our way back on our own."

Ellen grabbed her brothers by the arm. "Come on, let's go."

After ten minutes or so of steady jogging, they caught up to Hawk. When they suddenly reappeared behind him, he just kept marching along, acting as if nothing unusual had happened. They continued on a bit farther, until Hawk slowed down and veered off the path. He bent down, grabbed a sturdy stick, and led them up a steep hill.

"Where are we going?" panted Will, struggling to keep up.

"To the top of the ridge," replied Hawk.

"How do you know where to go?"

"I know all the routes and portages. I come here all the time."

About two-thirds of the way up, they reached a rocky shelf. Above the shelf, the rock rose straight up, much like the place where they had landed. Hawk walked up to it, found two handholds, and scampered up the rock face with the agility of a squirrel.

Josh climbed up after him. His first movements were easy; he moved his right hand and foot, and then his left. After that, things became more complicated. He stretched out his right hand as far as he could, but he couldn't quite reach the little outcropping of rock above him. He bounced up and down on his left leg as his right leg dangled in the air, until he finally caught the edge of the rock. Pleased with his efforts, he let out a little sigh of relief. Suddenly the rock he was holding broke off. He hovered in the air for a split second, not quite balanced. Little pebbles and a handful of sand dropped onto Will and Ellen below. Then, just in the nick of time, he leaned forward and locked his right hand onto a different rock.

Hawk looked down at him and shook his head. "You're too brave; you could have fallen. Keep three of your limbs in contact with the rock at all times. If you move one hand or foot at a time, you'll be much safer."

"Hawk's right. I was watching him; he never lost his balance," added Ellen.

Josh thought about Hawk's instructions for a minute, and then he lifted his right hand back up, searching for another handhold. Once he found one and his hand was securely in place, he shifted his body upward and searched for another foothold. His confidence restored, he smiled to himself as he repeated the pattern over and over again until he reached the top of the cliff.

Josh scrambled over the top and looked down. Ellen and Will were about halfway up, both doing remarkably well. Will flashed Josh a smile. "Look—I'm really doing it!" he shouted.

"Way to go. But whatever you do, don't look down."

A look of terror flashed across Will's face. "Why?"

"Because you're a long way up. Don't worry. You're doing great. Keep going."

"Are you sure?"

Josh nodded.

"Okay."

A few minutes later, Ellen and Will crawled over the top. They hurried over to Josh and Hawk, who were admiring the beautiful view. The lake spread out before them. It was sheltered by miles of jagged shoreline, small islands, and the occasional outcropping of rock that provided a home for the seagulls. Most of the gulls stood on the white-stained rocks, surveying their domain, but a few hovered over the water, looking for their next meal.

Hawk pointed to a marsh in a sheltered cove off to their left. They watched a huge bull moose wade through the tall rushes and lily pads that covered the water like a thick carpet, sending ripples in every direction.

"We never see stuff like this where we live. Boy, are you lucky," said Josh.

Hawk shrugged. He took ten steps back and then sprinted to the edge of the cliff and leaped off.

Josh and Ellen rushed to the edge, with Will just behind, and watched Hawk fly through the air, his body rigid, and neatly dive into the water below. When he surfaced, he waved. "Come join me—it's warm!"

Will stood there, shaking. "He wants us to jump off a cliff," he whimpered, his teeth chattering.

"How deep is it?" shouted Ellen.

"About four times my height. Make sure you take a big jump so you don't smash into the side of the cliff."

Ellen backed up twenty steps and made a wild dash to the edge of the cliff. She leaped off, screaming the whole way down, and landed with a perfect pencil dive in the water below. Josh followed a minute later. He landed feet first but couldn't resist using his arms to make an exuberant splash.

He and Ellen looked up and spotted Will peering over the edge of cliff, watching everyone play in the water below. "Come on, Will, you can do it," shouted Josh.

Will got down on his knees and inspected the rock face between them.

"You can't climb down; it's too steep."

Will stood up and walked backward until he disappeared from Josh's view. Josh was turning toward Hawk and Ellen when a flash of color caught his eye. Will's loud yelp disrupted the peaceful setting as he hurled his skinny body off the top of the cliff and plummeted to the water below.

Josh and Ellen were so shocked by his boldness that they gasped. Just before he hit the water, he let out a bloodcurdling scream.

They waited several seconds. "He's not coming up," said Josh. He swam toward the spot where Will had landed. Ellen was just a few strokes behind. The two of them dove down and discovered Will thrashing about, growing more panicked by the second. He was trying to retrieve his glasses, which were slowly sinking to the sandy, weed-covered bottom of the lake, but he couldn't reach them.

Josh looked at Will, and then at the glasses. Will was moving slower and slower. Fewer bubbles were coming out of his mouth and nose. He motioned for Ellen to come help. She swam over to Will, grabbed him under the arms, and dragged his limp body toward the sur-face. Josh dove down even deeper, grabbed Will's glasses, and swam back up. The three of them emerged from the water at the same time.

Will sucked in a deep breath and began sputtering and coughing. Once he calmed down, Josh handed him his glasses. "Are you all right?" he asked.

"I was really scared because I didn't know which way was up, and I couldn't get my glasses, but now I'm okay. The jumping in part was way better than the swimming part."

"What? You liked cliff diving?" exclaimed Josh.

"I didn't dive. I jumped."

Josh gave him a big smile. "Way to go."

The four of them were sitting on a rock at the edge of the water, drying off, when Josh felt his stomach growl. "Hey, Hawk, do you think we could eat soon? I'm getting hungry."

"Would you like some fish?" asked Hawk.

"Sure. Did you bring some?"

Hawk gave him a puzzled look. "No. We have to catch them."

Josh glanced over at his brother and sister. Will sat there, scowling. Ellen had turned a faint shade of green.

Hawk looked even more confused. "Haven't you ever caught a fish before?"

Josh frowned. "No. Our family really isn't into fishing."

"Well, first we have to catch one, and then we have to clean it and cook it. We fish different ways depending on the conditions. Come— I'll show you one way it's done."

Hawk walked along the shoreline until he found a log submerged just below the surface of the water. He stood there for a moment as he looked around and sniffed the air. Apparently satisfied with his spot, he walked into the water downstream from the log and stood there with his eyes closed. Several minutes later he slowly sank down until he was wet up to his waist and reached forward. He took two steps, his arms swaying before him with calm, even strokes, paused for a moment, and then slowly moved his arms together.

"What on earth is he doing?" asked Will.

They watched as Hawk pulled his arms toward his chest. When he stood up, water poured off him, but he didn't seem to notice because he was holding a huge fish, longer than his arms. The minute he lifted it out of the water, it started wriggling. He rushed to shore, hanging on to it for dear life.

Josh and Will ran over to inspect his catch. "Whoa, now that's what I call fishing," said Josh, admiring the fish as it flopped back and forth on the shore. The two-toned muskie was silver and a mottled grayish-black with spots. Its mouth gaped open, revealing a set of razor-sharp teeth. Hawk paused and looked up to the heavens. Once he had given thanks for the life of the fish, he opened his eyes. "If there's one, there's more. Why don't you try?"

Ellen cautiously stepped closer. When the fish suddenly flipped over, she jumped back. Josh quickly put his hand over his mouth so he wouldn't laugh.

"I think you should throw that poor fish back in," she suggested.

"Why? Josh said he was hungry. Now we can eat."

"It's hard to eat a fish you just watched someone catch."

Hawk frowned; his dark eyes squinted shut. "How else would we get a fish?"

Josh sighed. "Just ignore her. She has strange ideas about food. How did you catch a fish that size with your hands?"

"It's called tickling. When you find a fish in a hiding spot, like under a rock or a fallen tree, you stroke its belly. It relaxes, and then you grab it by the gills so it can't get away. It takes a bit of practice, but once you get the hang of it, it's really easy."

"That doesn't sound easy to me," grumbled Will.

The two boys followed Hawk into the water. Ellen watched from a sunny rock on the shore. Both of the twins found fish, and Josh even managed to rub one's belly, but when he tried to lift it out of the water, it slipped out of his grasp and swam away. Eventually both boys got discouraged and gave up.

Hawk found a flat rock and began to clean and scale his fish; he sent Josh, Will, and Ellen off to find some firewood. When they returned, Hawk was waiting patiently, guarding the thick fillets that lay in neat strips across one of the rocks.

Josh dropped his wood. Most of the rotting, moss-covered logs broke as they hit the ground. "Look at this great firewood," he said proudly. "I bet you didn't think we'd find wood like this right away."

Hawk let out a little cough. "You could say that."

"It was easy; it was lying right on the ground," continued Josh.

Will put his logs down next to Josh's. "Where are the matches?" he asked.

Hawk raised his eyebrows. "Matches?"

Josh nudged Will with his elbow. "They don't have matches—they probably haven't been invented yet."

"Then what do we do?"

"We'll let Hawk teach us how to start a fire," said Ellen.

Hawk didn't miss a beat. He walked into the woods. Josh, Will, and Ellen trailed behind. "I'll get the tinder. You find the kindling," he ordered.

"What's kindling?" asked Josh.

"Dry twigs—make sure they snap when you try to break them—and empty bird's nests, stuff like that."

Josh gave him a puzzled look. "But we just brought you some wood."

"The only thing your wood is good for is termites." Hawk walked over to a nearby pine tree and gathered a handful of dry needles from its base. Then he crawled under a group of low-growing bushes and grabbed some crumbly moss and dried-out leaves.

Once Josh, Will, and Ellen had each gathered a small armful of twigs, the four of them returned to the beach. Hawk sauntered over to the canoe and grabbed a smooth shaft, about the thickness of a finger, and a wooden board with notches carved into it.

"What's that for?" asked Josh.

"Starting a fire," replied Hawk.

"I thought you started a fire by rubbing two sticks together."

Will cleared his throat. "Sorry to be the one to disappoint you, but do you have any idea how hard it is to start a fire with two sticks?"

Josh's mouth twitched back and forth as he pondered the question. "I suppose I don't."

"It would take you hours."

"Oh." Then, visibly brightening, he added, "Hawk, can you show me how you start a fire?"

"Pay attention," commanded Hawk. He dug a shallow hole in the soil near the beach and arranged the tinder in it—the pine needles, moss, and dried leaves he had collected—along with a few grains of dry sand. Then he placed his wooden board next to the tinder, using his right knee to steady it. Next he inserted the shaft—the long, thin wooden pole—into the groove that had been cut in the board and began twirling it back and forth with the palms of his hands. As his hands moved down the shaft, it began spinning faster and faster. When he reached the bottom, he quickly lifted his hands up to the top and repeated the entire process again.

A thin wisp of smoke rose from the tinder. Josh cheered and slapped Hawk on the back, but Hawk didn't stop, not even for a second. He continued on, even faster now, until the smoke grew thicker. When a steady stream was billowing up, he dropped the shaft, fell to the ground, and gently blew on the tinder until it burst into flame.

"Yes!" cheered Josh, pumping his fist in the air. "Way to go! You started a fire!"

"Bring me your kindling," ordered Hawk. Will and Ellen handed him several handfuls. He carefully arranged them in a teepee shape above the flames.

Slowly but surely the fire grew. Hawk added more kindling until it was burning brightly. Once he was satisfied, he stood up. "Keep watch over it. I'll go get some logs."

"I can get some," volunteered Josh.

Hawk gave him a little smile. "I think it would be better if I went."

Once the fire had burned down to coals, Hawk wrapped the fish fillets in clay he had dug up and placed them directly in the fire. They sat there quietly until Hawk gave the word, and then they pulled the fish off the coals and carefully stripped off the clay crust. The scales came off with it, leaving moist, tender flesh behind. The fish was so hot that it burned Josh's mouth, but he was too hungry to care. Even Ellen, who was normally a vegetarian, managed to eat a small piece.

Josh sat there, fanning his mouth with his hand. "I need something to drink. Where can I find some water?" Hawk raised his eyebrows and looked toward the lake. "Oh. Why didn't I think of that?"

"Is it safe to drink?" asked Ellen.

Hawk cleared his throat. "Why do you ask?"

"I was wondering if it was clean."

"See that trail up there?" said Hawk, pointing to the path they had walked down earlier when they were looking for firewood. "That's an animal trail. Animals always choose the easiest route of travel, unless they're being pursued. Many animals come here to drink. If they haven't left any droppings, it's usually safe. Animals are wise about that sort of thing. They don't pollute the water where they drink."

"Really?" said Ellen.

"I'd rather drink from the same place the animals do. It's always safer than places where there's no sign of their activity. My father taught me that."

"Let me get this straight. Just because there's a path in the woods that you think some animals walk down means that it's safe to drink the water here?" asked Will incredulously.

"There's more to it than that. Remember the tracks in the clay?"

"I didn't see any tracks," said Will.

Hawk let out a sigh. "You sure don't see very well." He led them over to the spot on the beach where he had dug out the clay for the fish, and pointed to a variety of marks in the mud. "Those shorter tracks—the ones with the long back part and two smaller toes—belong to a doe. The longer ones are from a buck, and those really large ones with the two little lines at the back are from a bull moose."

"But what about those ones?" asked Josh, pointing to a series of tracks with small finger marks followed by a long flat line.

"They're from a fox. See that line where the clay looks like it has been scratched?"

Josh nodded.

"That's from its tail."

"Really? Wow, that's amazing."

"When you see a lot of animal tracks and no droppings, there's a good chance the water is safe to drink."

"They're very smart," said Ellen.

Hawk nodded in agreement. "Animals know a lot more than we give them credit for."

With their stomachs full and their bodies tired, the kids climbed back into the canoe and set out across the lake. As Josh gazed at the woods and the water, he realized that the strong sense of peace that had flooded his heart that morning had stayed with him all day. He let out a big sigh. "I feel like this has been the most perfect day of my life."

"Why do you say that?" asked Ellen.

"Because we've done so many great things. We made a new friend, had a canoe ride, went climbing, fished, started a fire, and cooked out in the wilderness; and Will and I haven't had a fight in hours."

"Why do you think we're getting along?" said Will.

"I don't know. There's something different about this place. Just being here makes me want to be good."

Hawk smiled as Josh continued.

"You don't seem to have anything—no video games, toys, or even books—yet God has given you everything you need." He turned to his brother. "I still can't believe you jumped off the cliff. That was totally amazing."

Will beamed from ear to ear. "I was surprised at how fun it was. I guess you can't call me a chicken anymore."

Josh looked up at the sky. "Do you think life was this great when God first made the world?"

"I don't know, but I bet it was this beautiful," said Ellen.

Off in the distance the sun was setting over the water, creating a thin red path from the horizon to their canoe. Josh sighed again. "I sure like it here. Where are we going now?"

Hawk kept paddling as he answered Josh's question. "We're heading back to my village. It's time to introduce you to my father—he's the chief—and the rest of my people."

— FOUR —

HAWK'S VILLAGE

CRITICAL DECORATIVE BORDER

T he kids were within ten strokes of Hawk's beach when Josh spotted a party of men standing in the woods. By the time their prow touched the sand, six warriors had their canoe surrounded. A strong, bare-chested man stood at the front; he appeared to be the leader. His hair was jet black, except for the few strands of gray that ran through his dark braids, and he wore a headband of eagle feathers. He looked at Hawk, grunted out a quick command, and grabbed Josh by the arm.

Josh grimaced from the pain. The man was squeezing his arm so tight that he had no circulation.

The man turned to one of the older warriors. "Are these the paleface you were dreaming of?"

The elder warrior nodded.

The chief looked at the other members of his group. "Don't let them escape."

"But Father, they are my friends," protested Hawk.

The chief gave him a stern stare. "Don't let them escape."

The warriors arranged Josh, Will, and Ellen in a line and paraded them through the woods. All they could see were the trees and bushes that lined the path.

"I feel like we're in the jungle all over again. This is not good. I might faint," moaned Will.

Josh managed to wiggle his way past Will and Ellen until he was next to Hawk. "What's going on? Are we in trouble?" he asked.

"Everything's fine. My father, Great Eagle, will keep you under watch until he's satisfied you're not a threat to our village."

"We won't hurt anyone."

Hawk smiled. "I know. You couldn't if you tried."

Suddenly the narrow path opened up into a clearing, and Hawk's village spread out before them. A domed wigwam covered with sheets of birch bark dominated the center of the camp. Many smaller wigwams surrounded it. People sat around in groups, attending to their chores. The women wore long sleeveless dresses of soft hide, tied at the waist. The men were dressed in breechcloths—long strips of cloth placed between their legs, pulled up, and belted at the waist. Most of the men and women wore durable moose-hide moccasins, but the kids ran around barefoot. Everyone, old and young alike, wore their hair in braids.

Off to one side, a group of women were busy making stew in birch-bark containers. They cooked it by dropping hot rocks into it. Other women were weaving large mats from rushes or sorting containers of berries. Their babies were propped up against the trees in cradleboards, bundles carried like knapsacks.

The men sat in groups around open fires, sharpening their toma-hawks, arrows, and the tips of their spears. They worked with a quiet efficiency, not hurried, but focused on the task at hand.

Great Eagle led Josh, Will, and Ellen toward the main wigwam and pointed to a log lying on the ground. "Sit," he ordered. He and some of his warriors disappeared inside the wigwam. When Josh looked around, he realized Hawk had vanished, too.

As they sat there, they watched life unfold around them. Two old men with white hair and deep wrinkles passed by carrying a basket of fish. They sat down on a nearby log and began to fillet their catch using thin knives made of moose bone.

Ellen turned so she was facing the other way. "I can't handle this. I'll never be able to eat tonight if I have to watch them fillet the fish."

"Me, neither," said Will, looking a little squeamish.

"Are you going to faint?" asked Josh.

"As long as I don't have to watch, I'll be okay." He concentrated on the patch of ground between his feet.

Josh spotted Hawk wandering through the maze of wigwams and campfires. "Here comes Hawk. I was wondering where he went."

Hawk sat down on the log next to him. "My father should be out soon. When he's done talking with you, I'll take you to meet the rest of my family."

"Why does Hawk keep talking to you and not to me?" grumbled Will.

Josh gave his brother a silly grin. "Isn't it obvious?"

Will shook his head.

"Because he likes me. If I were him, I'd do the same thing. I'd ignore you whenever I could, because you're a major pain in the butt."

"I am not," sulked Will.

Ellen grabbed both of them by the arms. "Guys, settle down. The last thing we need right now is a fight. Be quiet and cooperate."

"Yes, Mother," said Josh.

Will looked down and shuffled his feet back and forth, not saying a word.

After what seemed like hours, the chief came out of the wigwam. Even though it was twice as big as all the other dwellings, it looked like the slightest storm could blow it away. He motioned for them to come in. They followed his lead, ducking as they walked through the low doorway. Ellen found a clear spot, and they sat cross-legged on the bulrush mats on the floor. Josh look around curiously, wanting to examine the contents of the wigwam, but he was interrupted by Great Eagle's deep voice.

"How did you come to our village?"

Josh looked at his brother and sister, hoping one of them would answer. Neither said a word. He cleared his throat. "Um, we traveled back in time through the power of our God. We were probably sent here for a reason, but we don't know what it is yet."

There was a long silence as the chief and his warriors pondered this information. Finally the chief spoke again. "Does your God use his power for good or evil?"

Josh was so surprised by the question that he scrunched up his nose. "Why, for good, of course." He looked over to Will and Ellen. "Why would he ask that?" he whispered.

Ellen shrugged her shoulders. Will just sat there, scowling.

After another long silence, the chief stood up and nodded. Josh nodded back, and then the chief strode out of the wigwam, followed by his warriors.

Will looked at his brother and sister. "That's it? They sure don't talk much."

"If you only said the things that were important, you wouldn't talk much either," said Josh.

"Speak for yourself. I've got lots to say, and it's always important."

Ellen stifled a smile. "I see someone's a little upset. Maybe you should quit taking yourself so seriously."

"And maybe you should mind your own business," replied Will.

Josh let out a big sigh. "So much for not fighting."

The three of them wandered back outside and were waiting for Hawk when a young girl approached them. The front of her dress was decorated with a pattern of colorful porcupine quills, and two thick glossy braids hung down her back. She took a few steps toward them, stopped, waited for a minute, and then took another few steps. Eventually she sat down on the log beside Josh, not saying a word, and slowly moved closer to him, a little bit at a time, until their hips were touching.

Josh glanced at her out of the corner of his eye and moved away. The girl followed him. He moved again. The girl moved with him. He kept moving across the log until he was right next to Will. The girl settled in right beside him. Josh sat there, hemmed in on either side and feeling rather awkward, until Hawk reappeared.

Ellen ran over to him. "What did your father say?" she asked.

"The elders don't think that you're a threat to our village. You are free to come and go as you please."

"Good. Thank you," said Ellen.

Just then Hawk spotted Josh's new "friend." He gave him a funny look. "I see Little Bee has found you. I guess it's your turn to have her for a *worthy opponent*," he said quietly. "Don't worry. It usually only lasts for a day or two."

Josh jumped to his feet. "What do you mean? Why is she sitting so close to me?"

Hawk smiled. "A worthy opponent is someone who is difficult to deal with. They help you develop wisdom because they put your inner life to the test."

"What's that got to do with *her*?" he asked, pointing to Little Bee.

"She likes you, and she generally drives the boys she likes crazy."

"Oh, no," groaned Josh loudly.

At the sound of his voice, Little Bee stood up and took a step toward him.

"That's the last thing I need." Josh ran over and hid behind Ellen. He cautiously peeked around her shoulder. Little Bee was making her way over to him, one step at a time. "How do I get rid of her?"

"Josh, what kind of question is that? Be nice," said Ellen.

"Josh has a girlfriend. Josh has a girlfriend," chanted Will.

Josh lifted his hand to punch his brother, but before he could do anything, Hawk spoke. "Does anybody want to go fishing?"

Josh dropped his hand back to his side. "Count me in. Let's go."

"Good, but first we need to get you some proper clothing."

Within minutes the boys were outfitted in buckskin breechcloths. Will kept looking at his bare hips; he was used to having them covered by his clothing. Josh walked around, flapping his arms, shouting, "Look at me! I'm free! Free as a bird!"

Ellen came out of Little Bee's wigwam wearing a sleeveless dress. She ran her hands down the smooth, supple buckskin. It felt wonderful against her skin. Her dress was fancier than the boys' breechcloths. Little Bee's grandmother had carefully sewn a pattern on the front of her dress using tiny pieces of bone.

The four of them silently followed Hawk through the village, down the path to the water. Josh almost crashed into Hawk when he stopped dead in his tracks. The two of them stared at a dark, lumpy mound in the middle of the path. Josh watched as Hawk picked up a stick and poked at it.

"Move back, slowly," he commanded.

"Why?" asked Josh.

"These droppings are very fresh. There's a bear close by."

"A bear?" exclaimed Will. "Run for your lives!"

"Calm down," said Hawk in a low, soothing voice. "Walk backward, and stay away from any cubs."

Everyone was slowly moving back when a mother bear came up the path. She eyed them warily. Her chubby cubs ambled along behind, oblivious to the situation before them. They were more interested in sniffing the bushes that lined the path, looking for a quick snack of berries.

The mother bear pricked up her ears and lifted her nose, as if she were trying to decide if the people in front of her were friends or enemies. She took two more steps toward Hawk, then stopped and looked back at her cubs.

"She wants to eat us," moaned Will. "We need to get out of here."

"Don't run," ordered Hawk. "It'll make her mad. You can't outrun her. Bears are way faster than humans."

The bear stood up on her hind legs and let out a loud growl. Hawk responded by talking to her in a loud voice as he waved his hands above his head. "You don't want to be here; you'll only get into trouble. I'm much bigger and more powerful than you. Stay away. Go back to the woods where you belong."

The bear fell to the ground and swatted it with her paws. Her long, sharp claws left deep gouges in the dirt. She shook her head back and forth. Hawk picked up a large rock and stamped his feet. She replied by letting out another growl.

"Hawk, we need to get out of here," gasped Josh. He was so scared he could barely breathe.

"Keep backing up," Hawk ordered.

As they continued walking backwards, the bear nudged her cubs over to a nearby tree. They climbed up to the first sturdy branch.

Hawk glanced back. "Keep moving back, but whatever you do, don't run."

"But I want to get out of here," moaned Will.

With her cubs safely up the tree, the bear turned and faced Hawk. She pawed at the ground one final time and then lunged at him.

Ellen screamed. Little Bee disappeared into the woods. Josh ducked behind a nearby tree. Will forgot Hawk's instructions altogether and turned and ran as fast as he could. When Ellen saw him running down the path, she fled after him.

"Stop!" shouted Hawk, but they were too scared to listen. The bear continued running toward him, but he stood his ground, waving his arms. Suddenly, when she was about six feet away, the bear skidded to a stop, turned around, and walked back to her cubs as if nothing had happened.

Josh and Hawk continued backing down the path. When they were well out of harm's way, Josh let out a sigh of relief. "That was a close call. How did you know what to do?"

Hawk shrugged. "Most black bears are harmless. She was just trying to protect her cubs. I didn't think she'd hurt us."

By the time the boys reached the village, Great Eagle and a woman who looked just like Hawk were having a lively discussion with Little Bee, Ellen, and Will. When they saw Hawk and Josh, they hurried over.

"Are you all right, son?" asked the chief.

"It was just a bear. I stood my ground, and she backed off."

Hawk's father put his hand on Hawk's shoulder, looked him in the eye, and nodded. "Good," he said, and then he returned to his work.

Hawk's mother gave him a hug. She and Hawk shared the same thick, dark hair, proud nose, strong chin, and expressive eyes. "You should be more careful, my son. They don't always back off."

"I know," said Hawk, rolling his eyes. "I'm fine, Mother."

She smoothed his hair down and ran her fingers along his braids. "Sometimes you are too brave for your own good. Be careful." She gave him a tender smile and walked away.

"That's it?" exclaimed Josh. "Shouldn't your parents be more worried or something?"

"We run into bears all the time. They're not so bad. It's the moose I try to avoid. Trust me, you don't want to get one of them mad."

"I believe you."

"So, do you still want to go fishing?" asked Hawk.

Josh grinned from ear to ear. "What are we waiting for? Let's go."

Josh, Will, and Ellen followed Hawk through the village, down the path to the water. Even though Hawk assured him the bear was long gone, Josh found himself continually scanning the woods on either side of the path, just in case his friend was wrong.

Within minutes they reached the beach with the canoes. They passed them and continued along the shoreline together. Hawk handed Josh a spear.

He held it in his hand, turning it every which way. "What am I supposed to do with this?"

"We're going spearfishing," replied Hawk.

"Why? Wouldn't it be easier to do that tickling stuff again? That almost worked last time."

"Tickling only works when the water is shallow and there are lots of rocks and logs for the fish to hide behind. It's wide open here, so we'll try spears and a net."

Josh walked over to a rock at the water's edge, found a comfortable perch, and crouched down, watching for some fish. Hawk handed Ellen a net made of nettle fibers. She and Will sat down and began to untangle it.

"I don't understand why Josh gets to use a spear and I don't. It can't be that hard," grumbled Will.

"He's got better aim than you, and you know it," said Ellen.

"He does not."

"If you spent hours shooting baskets in the driveway, you would too. Basketball improves your coordination."

"She's right," hollered Josh. "I'm way more coordinated than you."

Ellen had almost untangled their net when she happened to glance over at Josh and Hawk. "Will, look!" The two of them sprang to their feet.

The two boys stood poised on the rocks, their spears clenched in their hands. Suddenly they hurled their spears into the water. Will was so surprised he jumped back. Josh's spear entered the water, but immediately bounced back up and floated on the surface. Hawk's spear went in and stayed there. He tried to pull it out, but it wouldn't budge.

Josh waded in until he was chest-deep and dunked his head under, trying to figure out what was holding Hawk's spear in place. He came up for a breath of air and went back down. Little bubbles drifted to the surface above him as he struggled to lift the rock that was pinning Hawk's spear.

Suddenly the spear began to wiggle and Hawk pulled it out. A tiny fish was stuck on it by the tail. It flapped back and forth, trying to escape. As Hawk pulled it off the stick, it slipped out of his grasp, fell into the water, and swam away.

"Good try, Hawk. You almost caught it," said Josh.

"Oh, Hawk, you almost caught it," mimicked Will in a high-pitched voice.

Ellen whacked his arm. "Behave yourself. I'm tired of your bad attitude."

"Whatever," he scoffed. He scooped up the net. "Watch and learn. I'll show you how fishing is really done."

Will boldly stepped into the water. The rocks just below the surface were covered in slimy green algae. He slipped a few times but always managed to recover his balance. When he was about knee-deep, he unfolded the net.

"Um, Will, what are you doing?" shouted Josh.

"Fishing," he replied. "I'll show you how to catch a big one." He threw the net into the water. It slowly drifted out. Once he was satisfied with its location, he sat down in the water, hanging on to one edge.

Josh cleared his throat. "That's an interesting technique. I didn't know you could sit in the water and fish at the same time. Where did you learn that?"

"Never mind. You'll see how well it works when I pull in a fish."

Josh gleefully rubbed his hands together. "This should be interesting."

He and Hawk continued spear-fishing as Will sat in the water. They saw lots of fish and other creatures, but they all moved so quickly that the boys' spears didn't even come close. Eventually Hawk caught one fish. Even though it was small, he kept it. He placed it in a birch-bark basket on the shore and gave Ellen the task of guarding it. Every time it flipped out she squealed and Josh had to go over and put it back in.

An hour or so passed. "I don't think we'll catch any more today. I don't know where they are. I usually catch lots at this time of day. Let's go back to the village," said Hawk.

"You did a great job. You caught more than anyone else," said Ellen.

Hawk turned away, blushing. Will didn't budge from his spot in the water.

"Come on, Will, let's go," yelled Josh.

"But I'm going to catch a big one any minute," Will shouted back.

"Hawk said it's time to go. We'll come back another time."

"Just one more minute. I have a feeling about this."

"Oh," said Josh, sarcastically, "he has a feeling about this. My brother thinks he has fish-finding skills we didn't know about."

Suddenly Will's net jerked. He stood up, clutching one corner with both hands. "I've got one!"

Josh and Hawk sloshed through the water toward him. "Don't move!" commanded Hawk. He grabbed another corner of the net.

Will pushed him away. "Let go! I'm bringing it in myself." The net jerked again, and Will fell headfirst into the water. Seconds later he resurfaced, sputtering away.

Hawk scanned the water. "Where's the net?"

"I let go," said Will sheepishly.

Hawk plunged into the water and disappeared. Seconds passed, and then a minute. There was no sign of him.

"Where is he? No one can stay underwater for that long," said Ellen.

Josh scanned the lake, looking for a sign of his friend. "Should I go in after him?"

Before anyone could answer, Hawk burst out of the water, about sixty feet from shore, gasping for breath. He had all four corners of the net in one hand, and he lifted it up as he tread water. "You were right; you did catch a big one."

He swam back to shore with the net dragging behind him. When it was shallow enough for him to stand, he lifted it up. A beautiful walleye, as long as his leg, wriggled back and forth as it tried to escape from the net.

Will folded his arms across his chest and gave his siblings a smug smile. "See? I told you so."

"I agree that's a big fish, but you didn't exactly catch it. If it hadn't been for Hawk, it would have gotten away," said Josh.

"I caught it," maintained Will.

Josh shook his head.

Hawk knelt down on the shore, carefully opened the net, and examined Will's catch. The fish continued madly flapping back and forth.

"This seems so cruel. Shouldn't we let it go?" asked Ellen.

"Let it go? This one's a beauty. She'll make a fine supper," said Hawk, clearly astonished.

Ellen grimaced. "I don't know if I can eat it after seeing it flap around like that."

Just then, the fish arched its back and flew through the air, landing at the edge of the water. Hawk lunged at it, but he wasn't fast enough. The walleye flipped two more times until it reached the water and swam away.

The boys stared at the water, a mixture of shock and disappointment on their faces. Only Ellen looked relieved.

Hawk stood up and shook himself off. "I'm starting to think the spirits are angry with us. Let's go back to the village. We'll try again later."

Just then Will looked down at his leg and screamed.

— FIVE —

ATTACK

H awk had just removed the leech from Will's leg and the kids were just about ready to walk back to the village when Josh turned to Hawk. "Do you like living out here?" he asked.

Hawk looked puzzled. "What do you mean?"

"Do you get to do whatever you want every day?"

"Not always. This is a good time of year because we have lots of food. In spring we move to the maple forests, and the women collect sap. We also cut birch bark for making containers, wigwams, and canoes.

"In the fall, we harvest wild rice in the marshes. It's a lot of work. My father paddles the canoe, and my mother sits in the bow and beats the plants with a stick until the rice grains fall into the canoe. Then we cook the kernels. Once they've cooled, we put them in a hole in the ground, and my father dances on them to loosen the hulls. After that we have to clean and dry them. I hate wild rice season, because that's all we do for days.

"Winter is a little better, because I get to go ice fishing and hunting. At night, we gather in our wigwam, and my grandparents tell stories about the old days. I like this time of year, summer, the best, though, because that's when we join the other Ojibwa at the summer camp. There's lots of fresh food, and I get more time to play. Most of the year we have to work, but summer is a time of rest. Our main jobs are gathering lodge coverings and making mats for the winter, as well as picking and drying berries."

"That sounds pretty good to me. I think I could handle a life like that. It beats doing homework," said Josh.

"It's good as long as there's enough food. If our supplies run low, everyone gets pretty grouchy."

Hawk abruptly stood up and turned toward the others. He looked up at the sky and sniffed the air. "We need to go back right away," he snapped.

Will slowly stood up. "Why?"

"Hurry. We don't have long."

"Why? There's not even a cloud in the sky. What's the big hurry?" asked Josh.

"We need to head back to camp. I don't want to be caught in the downpour."

Josh begrudgingly followed Hawk along the shoreline. Ellen and Will followed suit.

As they walked along, the wind slowly picked up. The sky darkened and a loud clap of thunder followed a flash of lightning.

Josh stopped for a second and turned so he could see Hawk. "You were right. How did you know a storm was coming?"

"Some of the people in my village can predict the weather by the song of the birds in the morning, but I just feel it. It's hard to explain, but I just know."

"What do you feel?"

"The clouds, the speed of the wind and the direction it's moving, the temperature ... even the light sometimes. I get a sense that something is going to happen. I can't really explain it."

"Oh. That's kind of creepy."

"It's not creepy; it's just the way I understand things."

Josh gave him a puzzled smile. "Okay. Whatever."

They were almost back at the village when more dark clouds came hurtling across the sky. "It looks like we got here just in time. I can't believe you can read the weather," said Ellen. Hawk gave her an embarrassed smile and looked away.

The wind picked up even more, howling as it worked its way through the woods. The trees swayed back and forth. Josh's bangs whipped into his eyes, forcing him to continually push them to one side so he could see. "We'd better get out of here. Where do we go?" he asked.

"You can join my family in our wigwam," said Hawk.

"Do you have any rules we should know about?" asked Will.

"Rules?"

"You know, rules about bedtime or meals?"

"We do what we want. If you want to eat, you show up at mealtime; it's up to you. If you're tired, you go to sleep. You only have to help if you're asked."

"Whoa, that's good," said Josh. "We need to get our parents on that plan."

Hawk was running up the path to the village when something caught his eye. He skidded to a stop and looked at the ground in the woods. Josh, Will, and Ellen scurried up behind him.

"What are you looking at?" asked Josh.

"I thought the ground looked disturbed," said Hawk, pointing to the forest floor, "but I must be mistaken."

"What do you mean, 'disturbed'?" asked Will.

"You know, like broken twigs or bent blades of grass, marks that someone was standing there."

Josh and Will peered into the forest. The wind pushed the dry leaves across the forest floor, making it difficult to see.

"Maybe an animal was there," suggested Will.

Hawk shook his head. "No, the signs are all wrong."

"Are you sure? Is everything okay?" asked Josh.

Hawk peered into the forest again. "Everything's fine," he said firmly. Heavy raindrops began to splatter down on them. "Let's go before we're completely soaked." He tore up the path. Will and Ellen followed him, but Josh held back.

He couldn't shake the funny feeling in his heart. He walked a little way into the forest to where Hawk had been looking and stood there in the pouring rain. Sure enough, the imprint of a human foot could be seen in a clump of moss. He looked around but couldn't see anything else suspicious, so he scampered back onto the trail and caught up with the group as they were entering Hawk's wigwam.

Will paused in the doorway. "What took you so long?"

"I saw a footprint in the woods."

"Are you sure?"

Josh nodded.

Hawk poked his head back out the opening, grabbed Josh and Will by the arms, and pulled them inside.

"Should I say anything?" whispered Josh.

Before Will could reply, a bolt of lightning exploded overhead, filling the sky with light. Hawk pulled the door flap down and tied it shut.

It was warm, cozy, and dry inside Hawk's home. The wigwam was shaped in a half circle. It had a domed ceiling formed by a series of sturdy branches crossed over one another and tied together at regular intervals. Large sheets of birch bark had been placed over the frame, thick fur blankets hung against the inside walls, and bark and rush mats lined the floor. Various belongings were propped against the walls: tools waiting to be mended; cooking gear; wooden pieces for bows that had been shaped, rubbed with animal fat, and were drying; and a stack of tree shoots waiting to be made into arrows.

Josh watched as Hawk joined his family—his mother, father, older brother, and grandparents—who were huddled around the fire in the center of the room. He and Will and Ellen settled on the floor across from them. Hawk's mother smiled as she handed each of them a birch-bark container of maple-syrup-flavored stew. It consisted of a thick broth with chunks of deer meat and vegetables from the village garden, and had a woodsy, smoky sort of taste. Everyone was quiet as they ate. Hawk was so busy wolfing down his stew that he wouldn't have been able to speak even if he wanted to.

Josh leaned over to his brother. "They sure don't talk much. We should call them the *quiet people*," he whispered.

Ellen caught Josh's eye, pointed at the meat in her stew, and then pointed at Josh's bowl. Josh nodded in agreement, so she picked the venison out of her bowl and dropped it into his bowl when she thought no one was looking. "I've never had stew flavored with maple syrup before. It tastes really different—kind of sweet like candy," she said.

Hearing their discussion, Hawk left his grandfather's side and crawled across the wigwam floor. "We've been using a lot of maple syrup lately. This year the harvest was twice as big as normal, so we flavor most of our foods this way," he explained.

When they were all finished, Hawk's mother passed around some bannock, a quick bread baked over the fire. The loaf went around once. By the time it reached Josh, there was only a tiny piece left.

"Sorry. I guess this is all there is," said Ellen.

"Oh well, at least I got the best part of your stew." He jammed the bannock into his mouth.

Ellen shot him a dirty look.

"Oh, that's right," said Josh. "I'm supposed to have manners." He spit his now soggy piece into his hand and took a nice bite. "Is that better?"

"Not really," grumbled Ellen.

Hawk crawled over to the wall and grabbed one of the tree shoots that lay in a pile. Josh watched as he ran a sharp piece of bone over it. Once he was satisfied that it was perfectly straight, he used a stone blade to cut two notches into it: one at the end that held the point and another at the other end, so the arrow could fit onto the bow string.

Hawk was sorting through a sack of feathers, trying to decide which three would work best, when his grandfather loudly cleared his throat. All conversation ceased.

Josh leaned over. "What's going on?"

"Be quiet. You must show respect when the elders speak. My grandfather has the weight of many winters on his back. Listen carefully," whispered Hawk.

"I have a story to tell," said Hawk's grandfather. He closed his eyes and sat there, absolutely silent. It looked like he was going off to another place in his mind. Will gave Josh a questioning look. Josh shrugged his shoulders and put his finger to his lips so Will would know to be quiet.

Hawk's grandfather opened his eyes and scanned the room, waiting until he had everyone's attention, and took a deep breath. "Many moons ago, there was a family with two boy foxes: a big one and a little one. They were the best of friends and went everywhere together. One day they were in the woods playing and they came across another small fox. She was lonely and wanted to play too so she joined them. She quickly discovered that she liked the little fox much better than the big one, so she became friends with him. This made the big fox jealous. He cried and cried, but there was nothing he could do.

"One day a bear came into the woods. He was hungry for fresh young fox, so he chased all three of them. After much running, he cornered the little vixen! Both boys came to her rescue. They nipped at the bear's tail and lured the bear away before he could take a bite out of her, allowing her to escape. From that time on, the three of them were inseparable. The little fox never played favorites again; she loved both friends equally." Hawk's grandfather smiled. "And that is the story of the three little foxes."

"But Grandfather, what does it mean?" asked Hawk.

There was another long silence as Hawk's grandfather looked at each person in the room. "Who can tell me?" he asked.

No one said a word.

Finally, Hawk's grandmother leaned forward. She was even more wrinkled than her husband. She brushed a loose wisp of gray hair from her face. When she spoke, her voice was surprisingly low and clear, despite the fact that her mouth had a sunken look about it. She had lost all her teeth.

All eyes were on her. "Three is better than one or two, for a triple-braided cord is not easily broken."

Great Eagle grunted in agreement.

"Heed her advice," whispered Hawk. "My grandmother is one of the wisest people in the village. She possesses the ancient knowledge."

After several more stories, Hawk's family took down the furs hanging on the sides of the wigwam and lay around the fire for the night. Josh spread his fur out next to Hawk's and closed his eyes. He was almost asleep when he remembered the mysterious footprint in the forest. A pang of fear gripped his heart. He sat up and fumbled around until he found Hawk's shoulder and gave it a firm shake. Hawk rolled over and opened his eyes.

"There's something I forgot to tell you. I saw a footprint in the moss on our way here. I thought you should know."

Hawk let out a big yawn. "I saw it, too. Don't worry about it. Coyote has been up to his tricks. It means nothing."

"Are you sure?"

Hawk didn't reply; he had fallen back asleep.

"That sure didn't look like a coyote footprint to me," mumbled Josh. He pulled the fur blanket over his chest and promptly fell asleep.

Josh was the first one to wake in the morning. He sat up and crawled out of the wigwam, being careful not to make any noise or touch anyone, for fear he would wake them.

Dawn was just breaking. The sun came up a beautiful orange-red, flooding the morning sky with pink and blue light. The lake was as still as a sheet of glass. He could see the reflection of the trees and rocks in the water.

Hawk stepped out of the wigwam after him. He paused for a moment with his eyes closed, facing east, the direction of the sunrise, and lifted a bear claw into the air. Then he slowly turned in a clockwise direction, pausing as he faced south, west, and then north. He continued on, lifting his face up and then down, and then he stood still, facing straight ahead, his lips moving in what appeared to be a silent prayer.

Josh crept down the path to the beach so he wouldn't disturb Hawk. The cries of birds filled the air. A flock of black crows swooped overhead, cawing loudly. The quieter twittering of smaller birds, as well as the chirping of crickets, was an audible reminder that the rest of the world was waking up, too.

Josh sat down on a large flat rock on the shoreline and looked out over the water. He took in the pale morning sky, with its white half moon that hadn't quite disappeared, and watched a pelican fly over the water, slowly descending until it landed with a splash. "Boy, it sure is nice here," he prayed. "Thanks for letting us come, God."

He jumped when Hawk slid onto the rock beside him. "When did you get here? You scared me."

"What do you want to do today?" asked Hawk.

"What are our choices?"

"We could swim, canoe, fish, hunt, go for a hike …"

"But what about breakfast? Don't we need to eat first?"

"We eat one meal a day. It's not until later."

"Oh." Josh put his hand on his stomach. *I don't know if I can wait that long,* he thought. "What about my brother and sister? I shouldn't just leave them. If they wake up and I'm gone, they might get worried."

Hawk sighed. "You sure know how to make things difficult. Hurry up. Go get them."

Josh skipped up the path. When he reached the village, he found Will and Ellen. They had just crawled out of the wigwam, and followed him down to the beach. The four of them were standing on the shore, discussing how many canoes to take and who would go together, when Little Bee scurried down the path toward them. "Wait for me," she shouted, waving her hands in the air. "I want to come, too!"

Josh looked over his shoulder and spotted her. "Oh, no, not her again," he groaned.

"Be nice," chastised Ellen.

Little Bee walked over to the side of Josh's canoe. She gave him a timid smile. "Can I go with you?"

"There's no room. This is a two-person canoe, and I'm going with my brother today."

"It's okay," said Will in a syrupy sweet voice. "I'll go with Ellen and Hawk. I'm sure Josh would love to take you."

Little Bee beamed.

Josh backed away. "There's no way I'm going with her," he mumbled.

"Josh …" hissed Ellen.

He ignored her warning.

Ellen sighed. "Little Bee, why don't you come with me?"

"Thanks. I owe you one," whispered Josh.

"So the boys will go in one canoe and the girls in another?" asked Will.

"We'll take the small canoes—they're easier to manage—but they hold two people each," said Hawk.

"I'll go with you," said Josh quickly.

Will frowned. "But what about me?"

"You can go by yourself. Do you think you can handle it?" asked Hawk.

"I've never … Oh, never mind." Will grabbed a paddle and stalked over to an empty canoe. "Just watch. I'll show you how it's done." He plopped down in the canoe and tried to push it away from shore with his paddle, but it wouldn't budge.

"Um, Will, you have to put the canoe into the water first," said Ellen. "See, like this." She grabbed the side of her canoe, pushed it into knee-deep water, and then she and Little Bee climbed in and began paddling.

Will's cheeks turned red. "I knew that. I was just testing you." He got out, gave his canoe a push, and jumped back in, causing it to lurch precariously.

Josh gave Hawk a knowing look. "This is going to be interesting."

The kids meandered their way down the lake. Josh and Hawk, and Ellen and Little Bee quickly found their rhythm. The girls took a slower pace so they could enjoy the ducks and loons. Josh decided that going fast was better than going slow. He and Hawk paddled like crazy, heading straight for a flock of seagulls. Soon the air was filled with a cloud of squawking birds.

Will didn't fare so well. He started out strong, except that he couldn't get his canoe to travel in a straight line. Soon his arms began to ache. Eventually he invented his own stroke. His newfound technique allowed him to travel in a relatively straight line, but it was painfully slow and he was always behind, sometimes even out of sight.

Eventually Josh and Hawk slowed down, allowing the others time to catch up. All three canoes linked together, side by side.

Hawk pointed to a thin strip of beach a little way away. "That's one of my favorite fishing spots. Want to go tickle some fish?"

"Sounds good to me," said Josh. They let go of each other's canoes and paddled over to the beach.

Hawk helped everyone pull up their canoes and stood there, poised, as he scanned the ridge of forest just past the sand. All was quiet; even the birds had stopped their singing.

Josh gazed up at the forest. *Something doesn't feel right*, he thought, yet nothing appeared to be amiss. He scanned the beach on either side of them. The water gently lapped along the shore. When he shifted his gaze to the trees on the ridge, he felt like his heart was about to leap out of his chest. Two golden eyes stared at him from the base of a tree. A large animal was almost hidden by a low-growing bush. Its long tail swished back and forth, causing the branches of the bush to tremble. "Hawk, get back in the canoe!" he hollered.

Hawk turned and looked at him.

"Get back in the canoe!"

Hawk gave Josh a confused look and shrugged his shoulders.

"Hurry!" screamed Josh at the top of his lungs.

Hawk took a step toward the canoe, but it was too late. An enormous cougar leaped out and sailed through the air, landing on his back. They fell to the sand. Hawk tried to roll over, but he was no match for the cougar. In a split second, it had him pinned to the ground and sank its four canine teeth into the back of his neck. Blood gushed out of the wound, pouring down his chest and back.

"NO!" Josh's cry broke the silence. He and Will grabbed their paddles, leaped out of the canoes, and charged at the cougar. It let go for a second and then bit Hawk again, this time shaking him back and forth like a rag doll. The twins hit the cougar with their paddles as hard as they could, over and over again. It looked at them and growled. Josh waved his paddle back and forth in the air, trying to appear bigger than he really was, just like Hawk had done with the bear. The big cat growled fiercely, took one more swipe at Hawk, and slunk back into the woods.

Ellen and Little Bee ran over. The four of them huddled around Hawk. He was covered in long, bloody scratches. The cougar's bite had left a gaping hole in the back of his neck. Blood pooled on the sand beneath him and trickled down to the water.

Tears poured down Will's cheeks, landing in little droplets on his bare chest. "The cougar was trying to kill him. He's going to die," he sobbed.

Ellen put her hand over her mouth. "What do we do?"

The four of them stood there, trembling. They looked at Hawk and then at each other. "I don't know what to do," croaked Will, "but if we don't do anything, he's going to die."

SIX

MIRACLES

J osh was standing there, watching Hawk bleed, when suddenly his thoughts cleared. "We have to get Hawk back to the village," he ordered.

"But look how much he's bleeding," sniffled Ellen. She grabbed Little Bee and broke down, sobbing.

Josh's determination inspired Will. He took a step closer. "We need to bandage his neck before he loses more blood."

He tore a strip of hide off his breechcloth and wound it around the gaping wound. They carefully lifted Hawk into the center of Josh's canoe. The girls boarded their canoe, and Will took Hawk's place at the back of his and Josh's canoe. Little Bee guided them as they paddled as fast as they could back to the village.

When they were almost there, Little Bee began crying out for help. A large group of people had assembled on the beach by the time their canoe touched the shore.

Hawk's mother took one look at her battered, bloody son and let out a loud wail. Three other women surrounded her and held her up. Great Eagle scooped Hawk into his arms and ran to the village. Hawk's grandmother met them in front of their wigwam. She spread the contents of her medicine bag on the ground. A small crowd gathered and watched as she wipe the blood and dirt from the claw marks in his back. As each spot was cleaned, she gently rubbed some powdered yarrow into his wounds.

Great Eagle carefully pulled the cloth away from Hawk's neck. Blood gushed from the wound anew. By now, Hawk's mother had made her way back to the village, and she let out another loud wail. She stood there, completely pale, her hands clutched over her heart. Hawk's grandmother quickly pressed a clean wad of crushed cattail root into Hawk's neck. Within seconds, it was completely soaked with blood.

Great Eagle groaned. "Summon the medicine man," he commanded. "My son needs a healing ceremony."

Within minutes, an Ojibwa man that Josh had never seen before strutted into the camp. Great Eagle picked up his son and followed the man out of the village to a circular, moose-skin covered tent in the bushes. Josh, Will, and Ellen followed and hid in the woods nearby. They ducked behind a clump of bushes and slowly stood up until they were able to see what was going on.

They watched as Great Eagle gently placed his son on the floor of the tent. Hawk didn't stir. Great Eagle backed out, and the medicine man pulled the flap across the opening. The chief lit several fires around the tent. Once they were burning brightly he sat on the ground.

Wild noises floated out from the tent. At first they sounded like animals: the cry of the loon, a roaring lion, a bellowing moose, even the chatter of a squirrel. A long pause followed, and then the medicine man began to sing in a strange chanting voice. They couldn't make out the words, but the eerie undertone sent goose bumps over Josh's arms and legs. Despite the warmth of the day, he shivered.

After another long period of silence, Great Eagle approached the tent door and thrust in a handful of tobacco. The door swished shut, and the medicine man began talking in a loud, singsong voice.

"Can you understand what he's saying?" whispered Josh.

"I can make out some of the words. I think he's praying to their spirits," said Ellen.

"Really?"

She nodded. "This isn't good. He's calling on the powers of darkness, just like the shaman did at the Mayan village. We need to pray."

They bowed their heads. "God, we know you have the power. Please protect Hawk from anything evil and heal his wounds," whispered Josh.

The last word was barely out of his mouth when the medicine man fell silent. The three of them looked at each other, wide-eyed. After five minutes or so, the medicine man started up again.

"God, please be with Hawk," whispered Ellen. Before she could pray any more, the noises from the tent stopped. The woods were completely silent; not even a breeze stirred.

The three of them looked at each other. "This is really weird," whispered Will. "What do we do now?"

"Keep praying," said Josh.

After another long pause, the medicine man walked out of the tent and stalked over to Great Eagle. "It is too late. Your son will go to the land of the spirits." He slunk away, leaving Great Eagle sitting there, his head in his hands and his elbows resting on his knees, weeping.

Josh pushed a branch out of his way and stepped into the clearing. "What are you doing?" cried Will. "Come back here."

Josh ignored him. He walked over to the medicine man's tent. Hawk lay on the floor, pale and still. He stepped inside, bent down, and put his ear near Hawk's mouth; he could hear his shallow breathing.

Great Eagle looked into the tent. "What are you doing?"

"Can I pray to my God? He has the power to heal your son."

Great Eagle stared at him, looking right into his eyes, as if he was trying to decide if Josh was trustworthy. "You have my permission," he said.

Ellen and Will walked through the door and crouched down beside Josh. He looked up at them with tear-filled eyes before looking back down at his battered and bloody friend. "Can you help me pray?" he said, his voice crackling with emotion.

"I'll go first," said Ellen. "Dear God, thank you for bringing us here. We know it was for a reason, even if we don't know what that reason is." She paused and took a deep breath. "Please heal Hawk, God. We know you can. Please show him and his people that you are the one true God, the only God we are supposed to worship."

"Please heal him, God. He doesn't deserve to die. It's not his fault that a cougar attacked him," sobbed Will.

Josh was crying so hard he could barely breathe. He scrunched his eyes shut in an effort to stop the tears. "God, please, please heal him. He's been such a good friend."

The three of them sat there, motionless, and continued to quietly pray. When Josh finally opened his eyes, he gasped. Hawk lay there, blinking rapidly. When he saw Josh, he smiled.

"Hawk, you're okay! God answered our prayers!" exclaimed Josh.

Ellen helped him sit up. "Are you okay?"

Hawk looked down at his chest and legs. "I'm fine. Why are you making such a fuss?"

Will frowned. "You were just mauled by a cougar, remember?"

"I was? Is that why I'm in the medicine man's tent?"

"A cougar almost killed you. Look!" Josh leaned over to point out the scratches on Hawk's back, but he couldn't find any. They were completely gone. He lifted Hawk's braids.

Hawk jerked his head away. "What are you doing to my hair?"

"But your neck … it had a really disgusting wound in it. There was a big chunk missing, and it was bleeding like crazy."

Hawk ran his hand over the back of his neck. "My neck is perfectly fine. You guys are the ones who are crazy." He stood up and walked out of the tent.

Josh, Will, and Ellen scurried out after him. "He's healed! Our God healed Hawk!" shouted Josh, pumping his fist into the air.

Hawk's father ran over to them. He wrapped his arms around his son and lifted him off the ground. The two of them did a wacky dance of joy in the clearing. "Thank you, Josh's God!" he shouted. "Thank you, thank you, thank you!" Soon the entire village had gathered round, and everyone was cheering. Hawk stood there, in the midst of all the commotion, looking completely embarrassed.

Once the furor died down, Great Eagle led Josh, Will, and Ellen back to the village. They walked over to the main wigwam. Great Eagle motioned to one of the logs lying on the ground. "Wait here," he commanded. "The elders want to speak with you."

After what seemed like hours, the elders emerged from the wigwam and sat down with the kids. There was a long silence. Josh could feel his heart pounding in his chest. It took every ounce of willpower he possessed to keep from fidgeting.

Finally Great Eagle spoke. "Hawk, stand up." Hawk rose to his feet. "My son was almost killed by a cougar today. You all saw him when he came back to camp; he was near death. The medicine man could not help him; we know his medicine was bad even when it did work. The God of the paleface healed my son." Many of the elders murmured in agreement.

Josh leaned over to Ellen. "What does he mean by *bad medicine?*"

"Sometimes people use the power of evil to do good things. I'm not positive, but I think that might have been happening here."

Great Eagle looked directly at Josh and Ellen. "Tell us about your God."

Josh glanced shyly at his sister, hoping she would answer the chief, but she avoided his gaze. She and Will both sat there, staring straight ahead. "Oh, boy," Josh muttered to himself. He gave Great Eagle a nervous smile. "Okay … Um … I don't exactly know where to start. Do you think you could ask me some questions?"

Great Eagle thought for a moment. "What is the name of your God?"

"He has a lot of different names, but I usually call him "Heavenly Father." Other people call him "Yahweh" or "Jehovah" or even just "God" … you know, names like that. "

"How does he speak to you?"

Feeling pity for her brother, Ellen joined in. "We have a record of some of the things God has done in the world, and the things people have said about him. It's called the Bible. It tells us about our God and how he wants us to live."

"What does it say about how you are to live?"

"The first part of the Bible has the Ten Commandments. They're laws that tell us about things that are important to God. They include things like only worshiping him, staying away from idols, honoring his name and your father and mother … things like that."

"Our fathers have handed many good laws down to us that they learned from their fathers. Our laws include things like treating all men well, not disgracing ourselves by telling lies, that the Great Spirit sees and hears everything and will reward us one day with a spirit-home according to how we have lived, and that we should not take another man's wife. All men come from the Great Spirit; we are all brothers. You and I believe the same thing."

Josh frowned. "I don't think so. Don't you worship the earth and the animals?"

"The Great Spirit is our father, and the earth is our mother. All living creatures come from them and are worthy of honor."

"But our God made the world, and he says we are supposed to worship him, not the things he made. Our God is kind of hard to explain because we can't see him, but we know he's always with us," said Ellen.

"If you can't see him, how do you know he's with you?" asked one of the elders.

"Sometimes I can just tell he's there, especially when I'm talking to him. We call that praying. When I ask him for things, he always answers, even though sometimes it's in a different way than I think he should. He sees and knows everything, including what's best for each one of us."

"I am pleased that your God allowed my son to live. Our spirit's power was not strong enough to save Hawk, but your God's was." Great Eagle paused. "I will think about this, and we will talk about your God again later." With that, he stood up, and he and the elders scattered throughout the village.

Josh let out a sigh of relief. "That went better than I thought it would, but boy, is it ever hard talking to a bunch of adults about God."

"You did a good job," said Ellen.

"Thanks."

"Want to go back out in the canoes?" asked Hawk.

Josh smiled. "Only if you promise to stay away from the wildlife."

The kids were wandering through the village when Hawk's mother spotted them. She ran over and grabbed Hawk by the arm.

"Where are you going?" she asked.

"We're going out in the canoes for a little while."

She shook her head. "You almost died this morning. You must stay in the village until we are certain that your wounds have healed."

"Look," Hawk said, lifting up his braids, "there's not a scratch on me. I'm fine. You let me go out all the time. Why should today be any different?"

"Because I need to keep watch over you." Her eyes filled with tears. "I don't want you getting hurt again."

"But, Mom …"

"Let the boy go," said a deep voice from behind. The four of them spun around. Great Eagle stood there, his arms crossed over his chest. "The boy will be fine. He knows to be careful."

"Thanks, Dad," said Hawk. He rushed down the path to the beach before his father had a chance to change his mind. Within minutes, the four of them were leisurely paddling across the lake in one of the larger canoes toward the nearest island.

The island had a large beach covered in sand dunes, the perfect place for landing their canoe. Just past the beach, the ground rose sharply, not leveling out until the rocks gave way to the woods. Three white pines grew in the center of the island, surrounded by smaller fir and other low-growing bushes. A flock of seagulls also lived there and had left their mark in various ways—numerous fish skeletons lay strewn about, and white streaks covered the rocks. They could barely see Hawk's village from the island. The smoke from their campfires was barely visible, but if Josh squinted, he could just make out their beach.

Josh and Hawk led the way as they explored the island. The two of them tried to climb one of the tall white pines that grew in the center, but there were no branches within their reach. All they had to show for their efforts were raw patches of skin on the insides of their arms and legs.

Ellen paused to admire the tiny evergreen trees struggling to grow among the rocks and the clumps of light green moss that made crackling sounds when she stepped on them. Josh liked the sand dunes the best. He ran between them, spinning out constantly.

"Look at me," he shouted to Ellen. He ran to the top of a dune and took a giant leap, sailing through the air until he landed on the sand below. "This place is incredible. It's like a giant playground. There's so much to do."

"It's going to take me hours to see everything," agreed Will. He had picked up a fish skeleton that the seagulls had left behind and was carefully inspecting its flexible vertebrae. A few steps later, he discovered the skeleton of a seagull. It got him so excited he couldn't stop smiling. He carefully removed its skull and carried it over to Josh and Ellen.

"What are you doing? Get that away from me," shrieked Ellen. "It's probably covered in maggots. You shouldn't be touching it."

Will held it out so she could get a better look. "It's fine, see? It's been picked clean."

"I don't want to look at it. You can't carry that thing around. You're lucky Mom isn't here. She'd make you to wash your hands with extra soap."

By the time they finished exploring the island, dusk was falling. After a quick swim, they settled on the beach for the night. Hawk built a small fire, and they each carved a hollow in the sand in which to sleep.

"Can we each have our own fire?" asked Josh.

"That would be too confusing," said Will.

"What do you mean, 'too confusing'? Confusing for who?"

"Three fires in a row is the international distress signal. If we each had a fire, that would be four in row. It would really confuse everyone."

"How do you know all this?" asked Josh.

Will stuck out his chest. "You need to be mentally prepared for everything at all times. I read a book on survival skills last year. It gave instructions on how to survive any situation: a plane crash, fire, being stranded on the ocean … You name it, it covered it."

"Okay, smart boy." Josh leaned back and listened to the sounds of the forest around him. The haunting cry of a loon made him shiver despite the warmth of the night. Finally his excitement gave way to a restless sleep.

Hawk woke with the sunrise. He sat up and shook the sand off his back and arms like a dog shaking after a swim, waking everybody up.

"Is it morning?" groaned Will.

Josh opened his eyes. All he could see was the clear, cloudless sky. "It's going to be a great day," he mumbled.

By the time everyone was up, Hawk had stoked the fire, picked three handfuls of berries, and caught two fish. They were sitting around the fire, lazily enjoying the morning, when Ellen decided to go for a little walk down the beach. She hadn't been gone long when the sound of her voice jarred the boys from their daydreams.

Josh jumped to his feet. "It sounds like something is wrong. I better go check on her." He had almost caught up with his sister when he spotted the problem: six large canoes were coming across the water toward them. "Hey, Hawk, somebody's coming. Are those people from your village?" he hollered.

Hawk ran over, spraying sand behind him, and peered across the lake. He stood there intently, not saying a word.

Will joined them. "Hawk, why aren't you talking? Say something!" he demanded.

Hawk raised his hand to silence him. He watched the canoes for another few minutes before he finally spoke. "It's a party of Dakota.

They know we're here—they've seen the smoke from our campfire. We need to take cover."

"What?" shrieked Ellen. "I don't want to hide. We need to get back to your village."

"Ellen's right. We need to get help," said Will.

"There's no time. Come!" Hawk sprinted across the beach and disappeared into the woods. Josh, Will, and Ellen ran after him.

A spine-tingling whoop filled the air, followed by a series of high-pitched cries.

"What was that?" panted Will, running with his arms clutched against his chest.

"Their war cry. They're getting close," said Hawk.

"That doesn't sound good," he moaned.

The four of them huddled behind a large rock. A flurry of cries and more whoops drifted toward them as the Dakota landed on the beach. Warriors poured out of their canoes, their faces covered in war paint. They carried spears and bows, and quivers of arrows lay across their backs. They ran over to Hawk's fire and then spread out over the island.

"What are those things on the sticks standing up in the back of their canoes?" whispered Josh.

"Scalps," said Hawk.

"From what?" Josh asked, his voice trembling.

"The last people they killed."

"We're going to die," moaned Will.

"We need to find a good place to hide. Follow me." Hawk ran deeper into the woods, toward the center of the island.

One of the Dakota warriors let out another loud whoop. It sounded like he was right behind them. Josh, Ellen, and Will ran as fast as they could. Within seconds they were right behind Hawk.

"Where are you taking us?" panted Will, struggling to get the words out between gasps for air.

"Once they've left the beach, we'll run back to the dunes. We can hide there. If they catch us, yell as loud as you can."

"Why?" said Ellen.

"Sound travels. If the wind is blowing in the right direction, my people might hear us."

The four of them waited in the midst of a thicket of saplings and bushes, breathless and shaking, until they heard several more warriors run by, yelling and whooping as they went. Josh, Will, and Ellen looked at Hawk. All the color drained from his face; he looked terrified. After what seemed like forever, Hawk gave the signal and moved soundlessly from their hiding place back toward the beach. Josh, Will, and Ellen followed as best they could, stumbling as their feet made the transition from the firm ground of the woods to the soft sand of the shore. Will landed flat on his face, but quickly got onto his hands and knees and crawled at top speed to the nearest dune, crying. He madly dug a hole in its side. When it was big enough, he crawled in and covered the opening as best he could, leaving only a small slit for air.

Josh, Ellen, and Hawk had reached the dunes closest to the water when the Dakota burst out of the woods. Their war party was made up of about twenty men, most in their late teens. Their faces and chests were covered in black and red war paint, and they wore feathered headbands across their foreheads. Their leader—a big, strong man with twice as many feathers as everyone else—shouted unintelligible commands, and the group split into two, one half going right and the other left.

Josh, Ellen, and Hawk ducked down, trying to hide as the Dakota methodically searched the dunes, one at a time. They walked right past Will without discovering his hiding spot and were getting close to the others when Josh had an idea.

He leaned over to Hawk. "Can you get us out of here?" he whispered. Hawk nodded.

"Good." Josh motioned to Ellen to follow him.

Just as the warriors were coming around their dune, they slipped away, ducking behind one dune after another until they crossed the beach. Eventually they reached the dune closest to the woods. "We have to make a run for the trees. If we can get back to the other side of the island, we can make a fire and send smoke signals," said Josh.

"Are you crazy? We don't have time to make a fire. Besides, smoke signals won't do us any good if the people who see them don't know what they mean. Hawk's people probably don't know what a distress signal looks like," exclaimed Ellen.

"Oh. I never thought of that."

"Besides, what about Will? Is he still hiding?"

"They haven't found him yet. It's probably best for him to stay where he is," said Hawk. He stood up just long enough to see the warriors. They were wading in the water, checking to see if the children had tried to escape by swimming across the lake. "The time is right. Let's go."

The three of them scooted up the ridge. They were almost in the woods when one of the Dakota spotted them. He let out a loud yelp. He and his fellow warriors ran across the beach after them.

"They saw us! Hurry!" shouted Josh.

Hawk fell back, letting Josh lead the way. He and Ellen ran ahead. Hawk shoved thin saplings and branches across the path as they tore through the bush. When Josh glanced back, he saw the lead Dakota jump right over one of the trees Hawk had just moved to slow them down.

"It's not working," he panted. "They're catching up."

After ten more steps, the Dakota were almost upon them.

"Hurry! We need to get back to the canoe!" yelled Josh.

They switched direction, making a large U-turn in the middle of the woods, and ran as fast as they could until they reached the ridge again. They managed to put just enough distance between them and their pursuers so they could attempt a getaway. With Josh still leading the way, they crossed the beach, grabbed the sides of their canoe, and half dragged, half carried it into the water. It was barely off the sandy bottom when the three of them fell in. Hawk began paddling with all his might.

Ellen turned and looked back. The Dakota were piling into their canoes, ready to give chase.

"What about Will? We can't leave him behind," she wailed.

"We'll come back for him later. Come on, Hawk, paddle!" shouted Josh.

Within seconds all six Dakota canoes were in hot pursuit. Arrows landed in the water on either side of them.

"What do we do now?" cried Ellen. "We're going to die."

SEVEN

THE
COUNCIL FIRE

CRITICOROROROROROROROROROR

Ellen's question was answered by the loud cry of fifty Ojibwa warriors. By the time they reached Hawk in their canoes, they had let off their own volley of arrows. The Dakota didn't have a chance.

The battle was fierce. Volleys of arrows flew through the air and tomahawks relentlessly chopped down. Fortunately, it was over within minutes.

The Ojibwa warriors leaped out of their canoes and dragged the dead Dakota warriors to shore. They stripped them of their weapons and beaded jewelry and laid them in a neat row along the sand. The sight of the bodies lying there was so horrible that Josh had to look away; he couldn't bear it. Just the thought of all those dead people made him feel sick to his stomach. Ellen sat beside him, sobbing. Everything had happened so fast that it was hard to believe a battle had really taken place. The fighting had been so intense that it was a shock to their senses. They watched as the two lone Dakota who had survived were tied up and dumped unceremoniously into one of the Ojibwa canoes.

With the threat removed, the Ojibwa rounded up the kids, including

Will, who had finally climbed out of his sand dune. One of the warriors grabbed the twins by the arms and towed them across the beach.

Will tried to pull away, but the Ojibwa warrior wouldn't let go. "Do you have to squeeze so tight?" he moaned. "You're hurting me." His protests ended when he spotted the row of bodies on the beach. The sight upset him so badly that he leaned over and threw up on the sand.

The warrior gave Will a look of disgust. "You have caused much trouble since you arrived. Come with me."

His words got Will's attention. He looked the man square in the eye, and then with a boldness that surprised Josh, he said, "What do you mean, *trouble?* We prayed for Hawk and God saved his life. You call that *trouble?*"

"We put our lives in danger to save you. You should be grateful," said the warrior.

"It's not our fault those warriors came after us. We were just hanging out, minding our own business, and then, boom, they showed up out of nowhere. We had nothing to do with it."

The warrior eased up his grip slightly and gave Will a patronizing smile. "We shall let the tribal council decide."

"What's a tribal council?"

Despite Will's persistent questioning, the Ojibwa warrior wouldn't reply. He turned to his comrades while keeping a tight grip on Will's arm.

The warrior didn't want to let Josh and Will travel in a canoe with Hawk, but he finally relented after Hawk promised him nothing bad would happen. The four of them climbed back into their canoe and floated in the water near the beach, discussing the Dakota attack as they waited for Hawk's people to finish loading their canoes.

"You know, Will, I still don't understand why you hid in that sand dune," said Josh.

"It was pretty hot in there," he agreed.

"What were you thinking? What if they had found you? You'd have been another scalp on the back of their canoe."

"What do you mean? It was a great plan. I was completely safe, not like some other people I know who ran around the island with a bunch of warriors chasing after them."

"We were running because we were going to make a fire and send smoke signals. We had a plan," said Josh.

"Josh, we nixed that plan, remember? All that running around almost got us killed," said Ellen.

"It did not. I was trying to save us. You know, it's hard to think when you're being attacked. I did the best I could."

"There's just one thing I don't understand. Why did they attack us in the first place?" asked Will.

"We're often at war with one tribe or another. We never seek conflict ourselves and don't fight unless we're provoked. My father insists that we follow that rule in our village. Sometimes I think the other tribes attack us because they're looking for something to do. It keeps their fighting skills sharp," said Hawk.

Ellen frowned. "That's crazy. Why would you want to fight just for something to do?"

"I agree. It doesn't make any sense, and it takes up too much of our time." Hawk picked up his paddle. "It looks like we're ready to head back. Let's go."

Within minutes of their arrival in the village, word had spread about the Dakota attack, and people began to assemble in the open area near the main wigwam for the "council fire." A large fire burned in the center of the clearing, despite the warm, bright day. The men of the village sat in a circle around it. A circle of women were arranged behind them. The children formed the third circle. Josh, Will, Ellen, and Hawk sat down at the edge of the group.

Josh leaned over to Hawk. "What's this about?"

"The elders called the council fire to discuss the Dakota attack. My father interrogated the two warriors they captured, but they wouldn't say anything, so now we have to decide what to do. Everyone in the village can give their opinion, and then we'll make a decision together."

"Do we have to say anything?" asked Josh.

"Only if you want to."

"Oh, good," he said, letting out a sigh of relief. "I don't."

Hawk's father stood in the center of the circle. He dipped a piece of dried sage into the fire. Once it was smoldering, he held it up with one hand and raised an eagle feather with the other, pointing them in the seven directions: east, south, west, north, up, down, and straight ahead. Then he went around the circle in a clockwise motion and smudged each person—he waved the burning sage over them, one by one, while fanning the smoke with the feather.

Once everyone had been smudged, an old man stood up, holding a fancy willow stick. The stick was about Josh's height. It was wrapped with green rope and decorated with pieces of fur and feathers.

"The talking stick," said the old man, speaking very slowly in a low singsong voice, "reminds us of the wisdom and knowledge of creation. The green rope reminds us of our prayer to the evergreens, who keep their color through even the harshest winds in the midst of winter." The crowd sat perfectly still, hanging on his every word.

"The coyote fur," he continued, pointing to a chunk of brownish fur on one end, "reminds us of the trickster in all of us."

"What does he mean by that coyote stuff?" whispered Josh.

"The coyote is a tricky animal—it does interesting things—so we use it as a symbol of the mischief in all people." said Hawk.

"Is that what you meant when you said the coyote made that foot-print in the woods?"

"Yes. It was probably someone from the village playing a prank."

The elder moved his hand up the stick and fingered some long strands of black hair. "The horsehair, from the animal that has carried us for generations, symbolizes how our prayers will be carried forward from here. The wolf hair in the middle reminds us to pray for the wisdom of the wolf, the great teacher of the animal kingdom."

Josh leaned over to his sister. "Is it my imagination, or are they praying to the animals?"

"I'm not sure. It's so confusing. All I know is that we only pray to God and Jesus."

"That's what I thought."

The old man handed the stick to the chief. Great Eagle twirled the stick between his hands, causing the horsehair to spin back and forth, and then he tipped his head back until he was looking at the clouds. "Oh, Great Spirit, show us what is right. Show us the path we are to take."

"Is he praying to the same God we pray to?" asked Josh.

"I don't know," whispered Ellen. "I don't understand what's going on."

When Josh turned to ask Hawk about this, he discovered that Little Bee had worked her way over to him and squeezed in beside him. He moved the other way until he was right next to Ellen. Little Bee followed him.

"Ellen, can we trade places?" he whispered.

"Why?" she said, not taking her eyes off the chief.

"Look."

Ellen turned and saw Little Bee's leg resting against Josh's. "Oh," she said, knowingly. "Remember what Hawk said about your worthy opponent?"

"Yeah," said Josh, scowling.

"Sorry, but you need to fight your own battles."

"Thanks for nothing," he replied, jabbing her as hard as he could with his elbow.

"Ouch!" she shrieked. Everyone in the crowd turned and stared at her. She turned bright red and looked down at the ground.

The chief walked over and handed Josh the talking stick. He reluctantly took it and looked around uncertainly. "What am I supposed to do with this?" he asked, chewing on his bottom lip.

"It is your turn to speak," replied the chief.

"Oh. But I don't have anything to say."

The chief lowered his eyebrows. "We will wait for you to find the words."

Josh gulped. He looked down at the stick on his lap.

"Stand up," ordered the chief.

Josh struggled to his feet. "Well, we were out on the island, and the Dakota attacked us. It was pretty bad." He paused for a moment. "They followed us through the woods, and … " His mind went completely blank.

"We ran back to the beach," whispered Ellen.

"Oh … and then we ran back to the beach, and they were still coming after us, and then we came back here after you rescued us." Everyone sat perfectly still, patiently waiting for his next words. His cheeks started to burn. "I'm, um … I'm really glad to be here. Everyone has been so nice, especially Hawk, and I really like your village. It's very nice. I wish we had a wigwam at home." He looked up and noticed he still had everyone's attention. His confidence grew. "The only thing I don't understand is why you only eat one meal a day. I'm not used to going that long without food, but I'll try to get used to it. Hawk's mother is a very good cook. She makes good venison stew."

When the chief loudly cleared his throat, Josh looked up and stopped his rambling. The chief held out his hand ,and Josh carefully placed the stick in it. It moved across the circle to a wrinkly old woman.

"*W'geewi-animoh.* You talk in circles. When you ramble on and on, it reminds me of the dogs that run wild and snap at their own shadows. You must change your ways or you will die like the rabbits that are hunted by the hungry wolves during the Hard Moon."

Josh looked over to Ellen. "What did that mean?" he croaked.

"I don't know, but it didn't sound good."

"She said you talk too much and it's going to get you into trouble someday," whispered Hawk.

"Oh. I've never had anyone tell me that before," he mumbled.

"Heed her advice. She is one of the wisest people in the village."

After a lengthy discussion punctuated by long silences, the people decided to seek a truce with the Dakota, but not until the elders agreed that the "time was right." A delegation was struck, to be led by Hawk's father, the chief. They decided to canoe to the Dakota village and return their two prisoners. When the council fire was over, some of the older members gave Josh a sympathetic pat on the head as they walked away.

"What does he mean by 'the time is right?' asked Will.

"We won't leave until the elders are certain that we can complete the journey successfully. If we leave when there's a storm brewing, we could drown. If we leave before we've gathered enough food and supplies, we could starve to death. Not doing something is just as important as actually doing it. If we wait until the time is right, things go a lot better," said Hawk.

Josh, Will, and Ellen followed him back to his family's wigwam. Little Bee was right behind them. Josh grabbed his sister by the arm. "Thanks for getting me into trouble back there. I really owe you one. That was one of the worst experiences of my life. Do you have any idea how scary it is having people listen to you like that?"

"Sorry, but you wouldn't have gotten into trouble if you hadn't elbowed me."

"It wasn't that bad. People listen to me like that all the time," said Will smugly.

"Oh, no, they don't," insisted Josh. "They were listening to every word I said without thinking about what they were going to say, because no one knows who's going to get the stick next. It's weird having people listen to you like that. You're lucky you didn't have to do any of the talking."

"I would have done a much better job than you," bragged Will.

Josh stuck out his tongue. "Hawk, can we get something to eat?" he asked.

"Sure. What would you like?"

"Anything but fish," replied Josh.

"All right. Follow me. I know where we can find something."

"What are we looking for?" asked Ellen suspiciously.

"It's a surprise. Don't worry, it'll taste good," said Hawk.

They sauntered down the path to the beach after him.

The further they walked from the village, the paler Will became. "Are we supposed to be out here?" he asked.

"My parents have a rule: After an attack, I have to stay within shouting distance of the camp, just in case there are more enemies around. Don't worry, we'll be okay."

"Are you sure?"

Hawk nodded. He veered off the path and led everyone down a narrow trail that ran through the woods, away from the village. Thick stands of white pine rose up to the sky around them. Josh stopped frequently to inspect the animal droppings that lined the path. He particularly liked the little pellets the deer left behind; they reminded him of malted milk balls. They passed by thickets of blueberries, their fruit still small and green, and a meadow of daisies and buttercups.

Hawk bent down and cupped the edge of a branch heavy with unripe berries in his hand.

Josh leaned over to inspect them. "I guess the time is not right, eh?"

"Why does everyone say that?" complained Will.

Hawk frowned. "Because it's true."

"I don't get it," said Will.

"The quality of our food changes every day. The sap runs only for a few moons. If we don't collect it at the right time, we miss out for the rest of the year. Blueberries like these are ripe later in the summer. If we pick them too early, they'll be hard and bitter. If we wait too long, they become overripe, and the animals get most of them. Hunting is the same way: The animals are the heaviest and meatiest in the fall, and besides, it would be wrong to kill them in the spring when they have babies that depend on them. The ducks fly away when the cold weather comes. If we wait too long to hunt them, we could miss them completely."

"Hawk's right; it's a whole different world out here. This isn't like going to the grocery store where you can buy whatever you want whenever you want," said Ellen.

"How do you decide when you should pick the berries?" asked Josh.

"The answer is different every season. We pay attention to their progress, watch the weather, and make the decision as best we can."

"That's enough talking, guys. I feel funny. We shouldn't be out here. We'd better go back," said Will.

"Why?" asked Ellen.

"What if that bear comes after us again?"

Josh rolled his eyes. "You're perfectly safe out here. Besides, everything worked out just fine. Hawk knew what to do."

"We barely got away in time, and you know it. That bear could have easily killed us."

"She didn't want you. You're too scrawny," taunted Josh.

Will stuck out his tongue and pushed his way past his brother so he could walk with Hawk. "Hawk, have you ever thought about going into business?" he asked.

"What's that?"

"Well, for one thing, you could get a lot of money for this land. Maybe you should think about selling some of it."

"What do you mean, *selling?*"

"You know, letting someone else own it."

"But no one owns the land. It was given to my people in a sacred trust for us to share. We take care of it so it will be good for the generations who come after us."

"But surely you don't need this all," said Will, spreading out his arms to take in the miles of untouched forest around them.

"The land is like our mother. She cares for us and gives us life. How could you sell your mother?"

Will frowned. "Hmm. I guess I never thought of it that way."

Their discussion was interrupted by a strange growling noise. Will stopped in his tracks and looked around. He couldn't see anything.

Another growl came from behind some bushes. Will spun around, his arms pulled tight against his chest. He couldn't stop shaking.

Hawk had an amused look on his face as he kept his eyes on Will.

The bushes near the path shook, and the growling became louder. All the blood drained from Will's face. He ran back and hid behind a large tree.

Josh sneaked out from his hiding spot and continued down the trail as if nothing unusual had happened. When he got closer to Will, he put his hands around his mouth and called out, "Oh, Will, what are you doing? You're going the wrong way."

Will peeked around the tree and looked both ways. "Be quiet! Where is it?"

"Where's what?"

"The bear. Didn't you hear it?"

"I didn't hear any bear. Did you?"

"It sounded like it was right behind me." Will looked both ways again. "Where did it go?"

By now, Josh was having a hard time holding back a smile.

"What's going on?" demanded Will.

"Oh, nothing," said Josh. He let out another growl.

Will stepped onto the path. "Why, I ought to—"

Ellen rushed over to the twins. "Will, calm down. He was just making a joke."

"It wasn't funny," sniffed Will. He wiped a tear from his eye. "Why can't you leave me alone? Everything's gone wrong today. I don't need you making things worse."

"Sorry," said Josh sheepishly. He looked down as he shuffled his feet back and forth.

"I just want to go home," sulked Will.

A minute later, they reached a mud-bottomed marsh surrounded by a thick hedge of cattails. Josh sighed. "Great, more fishing. I was hoping we could have something different for a change."

"We are," said Hawk. "We're cooking up some frogs."

"I don't eat frogs. I had to dissect one in biology. It was horrible," said Ellen.

"But we eat frogs all the time. They're really good," insisted Hawk.

Ellen folded her arms across her chest. "I don't eat frogs."

"All right. I'll catch you a turtle."

"Yuck! I don't eat turtles, either."

"Then what do you eat?"

"Do you have any vegetables?"

"No, but if you find some pinecones, I can roast you some nuts."

Ellen smiled. "Now you're talking my language."

Hawk showed the boys how to catch a frog. He used one hand to distract it and the other to grab it. They waded into the shallow water at the edge of the marsh. Hawk quickly caught two. He returned to the shore, paused to say a quick prayer of thanks, and began searching for wood for their fire.

By the time he came back, the twins were still emptyhanded, ready to give up. Hawk took a piece of buffalo horn out of his hunting bag. A wad of bark, dry moss, and rotten wood had been safely smoldering inside it as they trekked through the woods. He grabbed a stick and started to dig the stuff out.

"What are you doing?" asked Josh.

"Building a fire so we can roast our frogs."

"That's not how you did it yesterday."

"I know. This way is quicker. I forgot my horn yesterday, so I had to start it the hard way." Hawk dug out the last bit of the smoldering mass from the horn, placed a few small pieces of tinder on top of it, and ducked down and blew on it until a small plume of smoke began to rise. Then he crawled back two steps and blew even harder until the tinder burst into flame. Once the fire was burning nicely, he roasted his frogs and the pinecones Ellen had collected. When the pinecones were thoroughly scorched, he smashed them with a rock, splitting them down the middle, and removed the nuts.

Josh popped one into his mouth and chewed twice. "Yuck! These taste like nail polish remover." He spit the pine nut onto the ground. Ellen giggled as he tried to scrape the remaining bits off his tongue.

"Maybe they'd taste better if you added some maple syrup," suggested Will.

Josh rolled his eyes in response.

"Here, try a frog leg. Maybe you'll like that better," said Hawk.

Josh grabbed the burnt frog leg, lifted it to his nose, and took a sniff. "I'm not eating this."

"But I thought you were hungry," said Ellen.

"I'm not that hungry. What about you? What are you going to eat?"

Hawk handed Ellen some nuts.

"No, thanks. I think I'll pass," she said.

"We could dig up some cattail root. They're pretty good at this time of year."

Ellen looked at the tall cattails that surrounded the murky pond and turned up her nose. "It's okay. I can wait."

"What do cattails taste like?" asked Josh.

"If they're tubers, they probably taste like potatoes," said Ellen.

A big smile crossed Josh's face. "Maybe we could make them into fries!"

"Count me out," said Ellen.

"Me too. I'll wait until supper. I wonder what it will be," pondered Will.

"Probably venison," said Hawk, "flavored with—"

"—Let me guess: maple syrup?" giggled Ellen.

As they hiked back to Hawk's village, Josh's stomach began to growl. Even though he had eventually given in and eaten the charred frog leg, it wasn't big enough to put much of a dent in his appetite. Before long he was so hungry he thought he might faint. He jogged ahead, clutching his stomach, until he reached the other three. "Hawk, I really need to eat. It's urgent."

Hawk frowned. "Can't you wait until we get back to the village?"

"How long will that take?"

"I don't know; a little while."

"I can't wait that long."

"It will take me a while to catch an animal and cook it for you, but I can try."

"Couldn't we pick some berries?"

"This is the in-between time. The animals have eaten most of the raspberries, and the blueberries aren't ready yet."

"Oh." Josh looked over to a nearby tree. Wide pieces of bark had been stripped off its trunk, and its top was dead. A pile of two-inch long sausages lay beneath it. He bent down and picked one up. It squished easily between his fingers. Before long he had brown sludge smeared all over his fingers and wedged under his nails. "What are these things?" he asked.

"Porcupine droppings," said Hawk.

"That's disgusting. Josh, wash your hands, quick!" shrieked Ellen.

Hawk poked at one of the droppings with a stick. "They're very fresh." He looked up. There, perched on a branch above them, sat a nice, plump porcupine. He turned to Josh. "Do you think you can catch it?"

"I don't know. I've never caught a porcupine before."

"Give it a try. You can do the hunting, and I'll make the fire. I'll be right back," he added as he walked away.

"But … But …"

"Just climb the tree. Eventually it'll let go. When it lands on the ground, Will can hit it with a stick. They don't move very fast; it'll be easy."

A look of panic flashed across Will's face. "But what if it throws its quills at me?"

Hawk gave him a bewildered look. "Porcupines can't throw their quills. As long as you keep away from its tail, you'll be fine." He spun around and disappeared down the path.

Ellen shuddered. "I'm not watching this."

As Josh climbed the tree trunk, the porcupine moved up a branch. Josh climbed up farther. The porcupine moved even higher.

"Come on, Josh, higher," encouraged Will.

Josh climbed to the next branch. The porcupine moved to the top of the tree.

"You're almost there," shouted Will.

As Josh reached up to grab the next branch, the porcupine let go. It dropped straight down, glancing off Josh's leg as it fell. Josh let out a loud cry and clutched his leg. The porcupine hit the ground with a thud.

Seeing Josh's pain, Will decided to keep his distance. He picked up a large stone and slowly circled the wounded animal. Once he was confident it wouldn't move, he threw the rock at it as hard as he could. Much to everyone's surprise, he managed to hit the porcupine square on the head his first try. The poor animal collapsed, its quills sticking out in every direction. Will stared at it in amazement. "I don't believe it. I'm a hunter, and I didn't even know it," he gushed.

Josh gingerly climbed down the tree. His crying grew louder with every step.

Hearing all the commotion, Hawk raced over. "What's going on?"

Will proudly stuck out his chest. "I just killed a porcupine. If you ever need a hunting partner, let me know."

Ellen coughed. "I still can't believe you actually hit it on your first try. It must be beginner's luck."

By now, Josh had reached the bottom branch. He gently jumped down.

Ellen rushed over to him. "Are you okay?"

"What does it look like?" he mumbled through his tears. He pointed at his right leg. Six quills were embedded in his thigh. "I'm never going to get these out."

"Let me see," said Hawk. He inspected Josh's leg. "Hold still. This won't take long." He grabbed one of the quills at the bottom, right next to Josh's skin, and gave it a firm tug. Josh squealed in pain as the quill ripped out.

"See, it wasn't that bad. One down, five to go."

"It feels like you're trying to kill me," moaned Josh.

"He's just trying to help," soothed Ellen.

Hawk grabbed another quill. "No, please, just leave them in," begged Josh. "It's okay; I don't mind having them stuck there."

"They have to come out," insisted Hawk. Before Josh could protest, he had another one out, along with the last four in quick succession.

Josh sat on the ground, his face stained with tears. He looked at the six dots of blood on his leg. "Thanks. That feels better. What about the porcupine? Can we still eat it?"

"Of course," said Hawk. He bent down beside the animal, whispered something over it, and pulled out several of its quills, which he solemnly lay under a nearby tree.

"Is it my imagination, or did he just tell the porcupine he's sorry we killed it?" whispered Ellen.

"That's what it sounded like to me," said Will.

"Whoa, talk about respect." Josh struggled to his feet. "Hey, Hawk, why did you put quills under the tree?"

"We need to be grateful for the animals we take. They sacrifice their lives so that we can eat."

"Oh," said Ellen softly.

Hawk picked up the porcupine and carried it over to his little campfire. He singed its quills in the flames, skinned and cleaned the animal, and buried its carcass in the hot ashes. Once the meat was thoroughly cooked, he cut it into chunks using a stone knife, and passed it around.

By now, Josh was feeling much better. He grabbed a piece of meat and shoved it into his mouth. "Hot, hot, hot!" he said, fanning his mouth with his hand. The meat was rubbery and had a smoky taste, but it was better than nothing. Once everyone other than Ellen had taken their share, Josh gobbled down the leftovers.

"You really were hungry," observed Hawk.

"You got that right. It's so much easier to eat where we live. All we have to do is open the refrigerator door, and *voilá*, food!"

"It's a ton of work finding food here. We've spent hours at this today. I can't believe this is what you do day after day. I sure hope we can go home soon," said Will.

Ellen opened her mouth, but before she could speak, he added, "I know; it's not time yet. We have to do whatever it is that we were sent here to do. Then we can go home."

EIGHT

THE DELEGATION

The hike back to the village was uneventful. The kids arrived just in time for supper. Hawk's father, Great Eagle, announced that he was leading a delegation to the Dakota the next morning and asked the boys to join him. Hawk's mother fed them a meal of vegetable stew flavored with maple syrup, and then the kids spread out on the floor of the wigwam. Even though it wasn't dark, they were tired and promptly fell asleep.

Josh was in the middle of a delicious dream—he was sitting in the middle of Hawk's village eating a huge banana split—when he felt someone touch his shoulder. "Wake up, it's time to go," the person whispered.

"What? Mom, is that you?" Josh opened his eyes. It was just Will. He groaned and rolled away.

"Come on," said Will, shaking him by the shoulder again. "It's time to go."

"Leave me alone. You woke me up in the middle of a really good dream."

"I know. You were dreaming about Little Bee, weren't you?"

Josh grimaced. "No. I was dreaming about eating ice cream."

The wigwam door flapped open as Will went out, letting in a burst of cool air. Josh felt goose bumps rise all over his arms and legs. He sat up, got his bearings, and crawled out of the wigwam, being careful not to wake the others who were still asleep.

He lifted his arms and stretched, forcing his body and mind to wake up. The village was quiet and completely dark, except for the fire that burned in front of the main wigwam. The only sound that punctuated the silence was the occasional scurry of an animal through the bush. Josh jumped when someone touched the back of his arm.

"It's just me," whispered Hawk. "They're almost done loading up the canoes. Hurry!"

"Where's Will?"

"He's down by the water."

Josh and Hawk ran down the path to the beach. They reached the canoes as the last bundle was being loaded in. Each canoe had room for only two people; their supplies and weapons took up the rest of the space.

"I thought this was a short trip. Why are we taking so much?" asked Josh.

"We always bring gifts when seeking a truce," said Hawk.

Hawk's father barked out a series of commands. "What's happening?" whispered Josh.

"He just assigned people to their canoes."

"I couldn't hear what he said. Who do I go with?"

Hawk grinned. "Me, of course. We'll travel in the middle of the line."

"What about Will?"

"He's in the lead canoe with my father."

"He's not going to be happy about being up front, although I bet he'll be glad he doesn't have to paddle."

Hawk lowered his eyebrows. "What do you mean?"

"Doesn't he get to sit and watch?"

"No. He's the lead. He'll have to work extra hard to please my father, as well as be on the lookout for any trouble."

"Oh, brother," muttered Josh. "This could be interesting."

Will was fiddling with his paddle when Josh approached him. "Are you sure you want to be in the lead canoe?" he asked.

Will gave him a funny look. "What kind of a stupid question is that? Of course I do." He sat up proudly, his back straight and his chin jutting out.

"But what if we run into trouble? They'll see you first. You'll be an easy target."

Will rolled his eyes. "They gave me this position for a reason, you know. You have to be a special kind of person to get this job. I'm in the lead because of my exceptional canoeing and fighting abilities."

"Oh, really? I thought it was because your blinding white chest will act like a beacon, warning everyone to stay away."

Will made a face at him. "You're just jealous because they didn't ask you to sit up front."

Josh thrust his left hip out to one side, placed his left hand on his waist, and suspended his right arm in the air, like the little teapot in the nursery rhyme. "Hi. I'm Will, the super-canoe-man," he said in a high-pitched voice. "Just stick with me. My blinding white body will light the way as we travel through the night. I'm just so … so … so …" He paused, struggling to find just the right word. "I'm just so incredibly powerful, and everyone at Hawk's village needs me just so, so much."

Will turned away, but not before Josh noticed the tears in his eyes. "I hate you! You're a terrible brother. Leave me alone."

Josh turned and walked away.

The Ojibwa warriors traveled through the early morning light, watching for the slightest hint of trouble as the sun burst over the horizon and lit up the sky. Great Eagle led the way, looking magnificent in his shoulder-length feathered headdress. They hadn't even been gone an hour when Josh's arms, shoulders, and back began to ache. The ache quickly turned into a burn, and by the time they stopped for a break, he was so sore he could barely move. If that wasn't bad enough, his wound from the porcupine quills had begun to throb.

He hobbled out of the canoe, his legs half asleep from crouching for so long, and followed Hawk along the shore. The chief took out a pouch filled with venison and bannock, as well as a birch-bark container of dried raspberries, and passed them around.

Everyone sat there, eating silently. Josh leaned over to Hawk. "Why isn't anyone talking?" he whispered.

"They are visualizing what might happen later today. You're supposed to be doing that, too. Be quiet so the rest of us can think."

"But I don't know how to do that," he whined.

"Walk through the tasks you think you might come up against in your mind. That way, when the time comes to act, you'll know exactly what to do."

"Okay," muttered Josh. He sat there, trying to imagine what it would be like when they walked into the Dakota village. Instead of reviewing the various scenarios, he promptly fell asleep and didn't wake up until the chief cleared his throat and rose to his feet. On cue, everyone else got up and headed back to the canoes.

"Are we almost there yet?" asked Josh, struggling to get comfortable in his canoe.

"We're over halfway, but up ahead the current is much faster, so we'll get a break from paddling. All we'll have to do is steer for awhile," replied Hawk.

Josh let out a sigh of relief. "Good. I'm getting tired."

They had just pushed off from shore when Hawk's father and Will pulled up beside them. Great Eagle maneuvered his canoe so it was right next to theirs and gave Hawk instructions.

Josh looked at his brother, but Will wouldn't make eye contact. He decided to make the first move. "Hey, Will, how are you doing?"

"Fine," grunted Will, still looking the other way.

"Do your arms hurt?"

Will grabbed his paddle and gingerly lifted it up. "No."

"Yeah, right," said Josh, giggling. "I saw the way you lifted that paddle. Your arms are killing you, just like mine."

A small smile crept onto Will's face. "They are not."

"Are so."

"My arms are long past that stage—they're completely dead. I don't know if they'll be good for anything ever again."

Josh smiled. When he remembered what he had said earlier, his heart filled with shame. He looked away. "Sorry about what I said before. That wasn't nice."

"I'm sorry, too. I didn't mean it."

"I know."

Hawk's father pushed their canoes apart. "I guess we're going. See you later," said Josh.

Will nodded and let out a loud groan as he plunged his paddle into the water.

After more long hours of paddling, the Ojibwa delegation crossed the last expanse of water on their journey. Great Eagle and Will lifted their paddles into their canoe, and the chief unpacked his pipe and calmly began to smoke. Everyone followed suit. They joined their canoes together, floating in one compact mass toward the shore as they surveyed the Dakota camp before them.

The camp was set in a thin patch of scrubby oaks, on a narrow section of land only a few canoe lengths wide. Tall bulrushes lined the shore, their cattails gently waving in the breeze. They floated through the reeds until their canoes came to a stop at the water's edge.

They had barely touched the shore when a fierce-looking mob of warriors came running toward them, brandishing bows and arrows, spears, and war clubs. They surrounded the canoes, their arrows and spears aimed at the Ojibwa, ready to attack.

Hawk's father raised his hands up above his head. "I am Great Eagle. We come seeking peace," he said, his deep voice sounding louder than usual.

The Dakota lowered their arrows and spears a few inches, but continued to stand there, poised and ready. Hawk's father slowly stepped out of his canoe, his feet slipping silently into the water. He pulled his canoe onto the shore. "I have come to see my half-brother, Sitting Buffalo. Tell him I have arrived."

The mention of Sitting Buffalo's name worked like magic. The Dakota dropped their bows and arrows to their sides. The Ojibwa men unloaded several large bundles from their canoes and followed Great Eagle up into the village.

The Dakota village was large—almost twice the size of Hawk's summer camp—but was obviously a temporary resting place on their journey. The wigwams looked like they had been put up in a hurry, and most of their food and supplies were packed away. There was no meat drying on branches, no hides being prepared; none of the normal village activities were taking place.

Every eye was on the Ojibwa as they passed through the village. People poked their heads out of their wigwams and watched the delegation walk somberly through the camp. By the time they reached the council lodge, buffalo robes decorated with beautiful designs made of brightly colored porcupine quills had been arranged on the ground. Josh, Will, and Hawk sat down behind Great Eagle and waited for Sitting Buffalo to appear.

Eventually a tall man with dark—almost black—skin, a long nose, and a large belly emerged from the council lodge. He nodded at Great Eagle and sat down opposite him. The Dakota warriors took a step closer, standing guard over their chief. Great Eagle and Sitting Buffalo stared at each other for a long time.

"Is that really your uncle?" whispered Josh.

"Yes." Hawk gave him a dirty look for talking when they were supposed to be quiet, but Josh completely missed it.

"That's one big headdress he's wearing. I like the blue feathers. They must have dyed them."

By this point, Hawk was getting bored, so he decided to ignore the "no talking" rule. "They say Sitting Buffalo has the power to avoid capture; he hears voices that guide him, telling him where to go and what to do. One of his elders prophesied that no arrow would ever kill him. Ever since then he's been awfully brave in battle. He takes all kinds of risks that no one else would dare take."

They stopped whispering when Great Eagle spoke. "I come seeking peace. Some of your men attacked these children yesterday," he said, motioning to the boys. "These children did nothing to encourage the attack. It was groundless."

There was a long pause as Sitting Buffalo pondered his brother's words. Josh's legs had fallen asleep, so he began to wiggle in an effort to wake them up. Great Eagle turned and gave him a stern look. Josh could feel the heat rising up in his cheeks and willed himself to sit still.

Finally, Sitting Buffalo spoke. "I will instruct my warriors to leave your people alone." Great Eagle nodded and then two members of the Ojibwa delegation retrieved the bundles they had carried up from the canoes. One gift after another was unpacked and handed to Sitting Buffalo. There was a beautiful buffalo robe adorned with colorful paints, pair after pair of beaded moccasins, dried fruit, venison … It was like Christmas in the middle of the summer.

With the gifts out of the way, the two chiefs moved close together and began to smoke Sitting Buffalo's peace pipe. They talked quietly as the rest of the group watched. Once the pipe was finished, Great Eagle led his delegation back to their canoes to depart for the journey home.

Josh was sitting in his canoe, waiting for Hawk when he realized he needed to go to the bathroom. He climbed out of the canoe and ran into a nearby patch of woods. He had just found a private clearing when he spotted Sitting Buffalo and two young Dakota warriors standing behind a tree, talking. Josh stood completely still so they wouldn't see him.

Their conversation was low and stern. It looked like Sitting Buffalo was giving the two warriors instructions about something. Their eyes didn't leave his face. The shorter one had a long scar that ran across his left cheek. It bobbed up and down when he spoke.

When their conversation was finished, the chief placed his hands on their shoulders, looked to the heavens, and murmured a short prayer. He gave them a curt nod before disappearing soundlessly into the woods.

"Whew, at least he didn't come this way," muttered Josh. He stayed there, watching the two warriors as they talked. Eventually they turned and disappeared after the chief.

Josh looked around. *What should I do?* He looked in the direction the Dakota went and then down to the beach where his group was preparing to depart. *Why would they come out to the woods to talk? Something important must be going on.* He looked in both directions again, made a decision, and crept through the woods after the Dakota.

They moved quickly and were well ahead of him, but he could see a faint trail where they had disturbed the ground. Some of the leaves and grass were flattened where they walked through the underbrush. Josh was almost at the top of an outcropping of rock when he heard their voices drift toward him. He stopped, poised like a cat ready to pounce. Down below, at the bottom of a hillside covered in birch and pine trees, the two warriors pulled a canoe out from behind a large boulder. It was loaded with bows, bundles of arrows, several spears, and at least one machete. They pushed it into the water, and with a shove they were off, swiftly paddling across the lake roughly parallel to the route that the Ojibwa were about to take.

I wonder what they're up to, Josh thought. *I hope they're just going out to do some hunting—and not of the human kind!*

NINE

BETRAYED

The trip back to the Ojibwa village was more challenging than the trip out. The wind had picked up, creating whitecap-tipped waves that pounded against the sides of the canoes. Thankfully, Great Eagle was strong. He maneuvered his and Will's canoe through the turbulent waters almost single-handedly. Josh and Hawk had to work hard to keep up.

After they had labored for hours, the sun finally set and the wind calmed down. Great Eagle guided their canoes to the island where they had stopped on an earlier trip. He studied the area, making sure there was no danger, while the others set up camp. Hawk grabbed a fishing pole made from a wooden stick and walked along the shore. Josh and Will trailed behind, exhausted. When he found a spot that seemed right, he stood on a flat rock in ankle-deep water and cast out his line. Within no time, he brought in ten small walleye.

Hawk pulled a knife out of his hunting bag and efficiently filleted the fish with long, smooth strokes. Josh and Will dipped the fillets in the lake to wash them off and helped him carry them up to the camp. Great Eagle and one of his men cooked them over the campfire.

The men sat around the fire and ate the small but satisfying meal. Josh patted his stomach. "Boy, that fish was sure good. It's the best food I've ever eaten."

"That's what you said about the food Puma's mother made in the jungle, and about the feast we had in England, and about the food Pepik's sister cooked for us in Prague. Make up your mind. Which one is it?" grumbled Will.

Josh sat there, thinking. "I don't know. I guess they were all good, but this fish is especially good, probably because it's so fresh."

"All I'll say is this: It's a good thing Ellen's not here, because if she saw all those fish guts, there's no way she'd be able to eat."

Josh grinned. "That's our sister. I sure hope she'll tell Little Bee to leave me alone. I'm sick and tired of her following me around all the time."

"I bet she's telling her how great you are and that she should marry you," said Will.

Josh looked at him, bug-eyed. "Do you really think she'd really say that?"

"No," replied Will, laughing. "Little Bee should marry Hawk. I'm just getting you back for that bear noise you made yesterday. Ellen's probably not talking about you at all."

"Oh," said Josh. He looked disappointed.

"I can't marry Little Bee because we're from the same clan, but either of you could definitely marry her," said Hawk.

"What's a clan?" asked Will.

"It's a family grouping. My clan is the bear clan. We are strong, brave warriors who patrol our villages."

Will looked impressed. "If I were in a clan, what clan would it be?"

Hawk thought for a moment. "You'd be in the fish clan."

"Why? He's a lousy swimmer," said Josh.

"The fish clan has great speakers and scholars. They help people learn."

Josh scratched his head. "I guess that makes sense. Maybe that's why Will likes school so much. What about Ellen?"

"She'd be in the hoof clan. They are gentle and take care of others in the community."

"That fits her. What about me?"

"You'd be in the sucker clan," said Hawk.

Josh's eyes widened in surprise and Will burst out laughing.

"The what?" he exclaimed. "Why? No, wait. Don't answer that."

"But the sucker clan is good," insisted Hawk, looking puzzled.

"I want to be part of a clan that has a strong, powerful animal, not a sucker, whatever that is," grumbled Josh.

As the sky grew darker, Great Eagle added several logs to the fire. Their group huddled around it, enjoying the sense of security the flames brought against the dark, uncertain night. Great Eagle's eyes gleamed brightly as he shared the legend of Nanabozho, the first man who helped the Great Spirit, Gitchi-Manitou, create the world.

"Nanabozho's stride was so long that he could step across the widest rivers and lakes with one step. He was so powerful that he could grab lightning bolts with his hands, and his voice was like the roar of the lake in a storm. He could transform himself into any animal or anything in all of nature. When the animals schemed against the human race, he took the gift of speech away from them. He was the one who brought our people their first fire and taught them how to make weapons, how to hunt and fish with nets, plant gardens, and make maple sap into syrup. He also showed us how to paint rocks as well as our faces before going to war." The men sitting around the circle murmured in agreement.

After the long day, the crackling of the fire and the flickering of the flames was soothing. As Josh sat there, listening to Great Eagle's stories, his eyes kept drooping shut. Everything went fuzzy and his mouth hung open. Great Eagle happened to be looking at him when he suddenly woke up and jerked his head back.

Josh blinked rapidly, trying to get his bearings. The chief smiled. "You are tired. It is time to sleep. We will return to the village in the morning."

"Oh, good," said Josh. Within seconds Josh was curled up on his side, fast asleep.

Josh woke up in the middle of the night. The cry of a loon sent a shiver down his spine. He sat up and looked around, but the fire had burned to embers and the moon was hidden behind some clouds, making it difficult to see. Everyone was sprawled out around the coals, sleeping, including the warrior who was supposed to be keeping watch. He was sitting on the ground, leaning against a tree stump, his chin resting on his chest as he snored away.

A movement in the water caught Josh's attention. The lake was calm except for two stubby logs that were slowly drifting toward the shore. They were about twenty canoe lengths away and were floating perfectly in line with one another, about a yard apart.

Something doesn't look right. Josh crept away from the fire and walked to the edge of the campsite so he could get a better look. As he stood there, he realized what it was that was troubling him: a slight wake rippled from behind the logs. He squinted, checking to make sure he wasn't imagining things. *Maybe some beavers are pushing them.* He tried to spot a furry head or flat tail, but there was nothing.

By now, the logs were even closer, only fifteen canoe lengths from shore. *Okay, there must be some other animal swimming behind them. Maybe it's a gigantic fish.* He shook his head. *A fish couldn't move a log that big. What is it?*

Just then, something that looked like the heel of a person's foot poked out of the water behind one of the logs. Josh crept forward, straining to see in the dark. As the logs got closer to the beach, they slowed down, until finally they were only one canoe length away. Josh crept forward, hid behind a tree, and peered around its side, his hands resting on the sticky bark.

As he watched, two faces lifted halfway out of the water. One of them had a long scar across its cheek.

He spun around and ran through the bush back to the campfire. "Wake up," he shouted. "Someone's coming!"

Great Eagle was moving toward the beach before the night watchman had time to open his eyes. Hawk grabbed a bow and a sheath of arrows and ran after his father. The rest of the group grabbed their weapons and spread out around the camp.

Following Hawk's lead, Josh grabbed a tomahawk and ran toward the beach. Great Eagle was already there, standing in knee-deep water as he examined the logs, which had begun to drift aimlessly apart. Josh had almost reached Great Eagle when he heard him gasp. The chief fell and was dragged underwater. He thrashed about, sending streams of water everywhere.

Hawk let out a fierce cry, Josh screamed for help, and Will ran and hid behind a nearby tree. The rest of the group ran into the water, trying to help their leader. In the midst of the commotion, it was hard to figure out what was actually happening, but it looked like Hawk's people were getting hit over the head with clubs and collapsing into the water, unconscious.

Josh ran in to help, but before he got too far, Hawk grabbed him by the arm and pulled him back onto the beach. "Wait. We never do anything without a plan."

"But they need us," wailed Josh. "Look!" Half of the Ojibwa were floating in the water facedown, while the rest continued splashing about.

Will came up from behind. "We're getting clobbered. We should get help. Do you know the way home?"

"Of course," said Hawk. He and the twins sprinted down the beach, trying to stay clear of the fighting. Hawk pulled the first canoe they reached into the water. The three of them jumped in and quietly paddled away from the island. In all the commotion, no one noticed they had left. About ten strokes later, they were out of sight and madly paddling home.

As they surged across the lake, there was just enough breeze to keep them cool, but not so much that it slowed them down. The moon was bright enough to help them navigate, but not so light that it revealed their position. Even though their muscles ached from their long day of paddling, Josh and Hawk moved at an amazing speed. Will sat in the middle watching for trouble. There was a lot at stake; they knew that the sooner they got help, the better.

As they zipped along, a thin mist began to rise up around them. The closer they got to home, the thicker it grew, until it was so dense that they couldn't see a yard in front of them.

Suddenly Will leaned forward and grabbed Josh's arm.

"What?" Josh grunted. "You're breaking my rhythm."

"Stop! I heard something."

Hawk stopped paddling and straightened up. He lifted his chin as he strained to hear the sound that had worried Will. The voices of a group of men singing drifted through the fog toward them.

"I can hear them. Who is that?" whispered Josh.

Hawk grimaced. "That's a Dakota scalping song. They sound confident; they must be on the move."

"Those were Dakota at the island. I recognized one of them; he had a scar on his face," said Josh.

"Those were Dakota?" exclaimed Will. "I thought they made a truce with your father."

Hawk looked perturbed. "So did I."

The singing grew louder. "Are they coming this way?" asked Josh.

"I think so," said Hawk.

"What do we do now? I don't want to get scalped," whispered Will.

"Just wait. I'm thinking." Hawk lay his paddle across the canoe and sat absolutely still, his eyes closed and his hands in his lap.

Will looked at Josh. "Shouldn't we be doing something?"

"Just give him a minute."

The twins sat there, trying to stay calm, but it was difficult. The singing grew louder. It was interspersed by the occasional defiant war whoop, but there was still no sign of the Dakota.

Will turned to Hawk. "Hurry up! We have to do something."

Hawk ignored him and continued to sit there, motionless.

"Okay, fine," said Will. He stood up. The canoe rocked back and forth as he reached for Hawk's paddle.

"No! The time must be right," insisted Hawk. He grabbed his paddle from Will just as a small Dakota canoe emerged through the mist beside them.

Will fell to his seat and let out a bloodcurdling scream. The Dakota warriors were so surprised to come across the boys that they jumped up and almost tipped their own canoe.

"Help! They're going to scalp us!" shouted Will.

Hawk dug his paddle into the water. They surged forward. Josh quickly joined in. They managed to put a little distance between their canoe and the Dakota before their enemies realized what was going on. Josh could hear their leader shout a series of commands.

Josh and Hawk continued to paddle with all their might. The fog was so dense that droplets of water formed on their skin. They looked like they had been caught in the rain.

"I can't see anything. How many of them are there?" whispered Josh.

"You don't want to know," panted Hawk as he strained onward.

"No, really, how many are there?"

"They've been known to travel with fifty canoes."

"Fifty?" groaned Will. "We're dead. Maybe we should surrender right now."

"We're not surrendering. I've got a plan," said Hawk.

"What is it?" Josh's paddle hung in the air as he waited for Hawk's reply.

"Keep paddling!" ordered Hawk.

"Sorry!"

"Just past my village there's a river with several sets of rapids. We need to divert the Dakota down it. We have to go by the village first, but I'm hoping they won't see it through the fog. The rapids aren't too bad until you get further down the river. The current there is strong—it runs through an area called 'the Gap' that's treacherous. If we can make it through the first set of rapids, we can hide in an eddy just before the Gap. The current will naturally draw them past us. If they make it that far, the rapids will take them a long way down the river, far from my village, before it eases up enough for them to make their way to shore."

"But won't the current take us, too?" asked Will, his head spinning as he scoured the water for the Dakota.

"Not if we're lucky. Josh, I'll warn you when we're getting close. When I give the command, switch your paddle to the left, and paddle hard. I'll back paddle, and we should be able to make a sharp right. It won't be easy, but it's the only plan I've got."

Will pulled his arms to his chest. He couldn't stop shaking. "I don't like this plan at all. If we don't make that turn, we're goners."

"Can you think of something better?" asked Josh.

"No."

"Then be quiet."

Will turned and looked behind them. The fog had lifted slightly. In the faint light of dawn, the prow of a Dakota canoe was visible just behind them. "They're gaining on us!" he gasped.

"Paddle harder," ordered Hawk. Out of the mist, land appeared on both sides of them. "We're almost there!"

The water grew more and more turbulent. As they crossed the place where the lake emptied into the river, the water turned into fierce rapids. Huge boulders sprang up on either side of them, forcing Hawk to use every bit of skill he possessed to navigate.

Will shifted his weight and leaned to one side so he could see what was ahead. "Get down. Keep your weight centered, and stay low in the canoe," shouted Hawk.

Will plopped back down and started to cry. "I've never been in rapids before. What if we tip?"

"You can swim."

"Not very well. What do I do if I make it to shore?"

"Run upstream to the village."

As they moved down the rapids, the river narrowed, and the current picked up speed. It boiled and churned around the rocks and fallen trees. Two large boulders loomed before them. Josh looked back at Hawk, his face a mask of fear.

"Keep going!" shouted Hawk. He steered them toward the rock on their left.

"We're going to crash," shouted Josh. An intense pain seized his stomach. "God, help us!"

"Keep paddling!" shouted Hawk.

Just when it looked like the prow of their canoe was going to smash into the rock, Josh felt a wave of peace flood his heart. A quiet voice whispered, "*I am with you.*" They veered to the right and shot between the two rocks, their canoe sailing through the air as the water fell away under them, and landed with a thud in the swirling whirlpool below the waterfall.

Josh stopped paddling and grabbed the side of the canoe.

"Paddle!" shouted Hawk.

The boys thrust their paddles into the water and pulled back with all their might. They crept forward.

"Stroke!" shouted Hawk. Josh paddled hard again.

"One more time!" Josh and Hawk moved in perfect synchronization. The canoe popped out of the whirlpool and continued moving downstream.

Josh looked back just in time to see the first Dakota canoe come shooting over the falls. It went sailing through the air and landed in the whirlpool, but they lost their balance and tipped. Their canoe floated away upside down, and the warriors bobbed along, fighting with the current as they tried to avoid the rocks.

"They're not that far behind us. Where's that spot you were talking about before?" asked Josh.

"It's up ahead. Let's go!"

The two boys surged forward with renewed determination. Will sat on the floor in the center of the canoe, clenching both sides as he shook like a leaf.

The water around them grew furious again. Specks of white froth tipped the waves as the speed of the current increased.

Josh turned around. Five more Dakota canoes had made it over the waterfall and were gaining on them. "Hawk, they're right behind us!"

"We're almost there. When we reach that boulder up ahead, paddle on the left as hard as you can!" shouted Hawk.

Josh could barely hear him through all the whooping and shouting from behind. He looked around wildly and located the boulder seconds before they reached it.

"Now!" shouted Hawk as he held his paddle beneath the turbulent water and pivoted the canoe to the right. "Paddle hard!"

He and Josh switched sides instantly and dug their paddles into the water. For a long moment it seemed as if the canoe wasn't moving forward, only sideways as they were swept down the river. But two strokes later they had broken out of the current and entered the calm water of the inlet.

Josh let out a sigh of relief and rubbed his trembling arms.

"Look!" exclaimed Will. They watched as the current swept one Dakota canoe after another past them. Their warriors looked completely bewildered as their canoes were dragged downstream.

Hawk raised his eyes to the heavens. His lips moved in silent prayer. Josh gave Will a guilty smile, and the two of them bowed their heads and prayed.

"What do we do now? What if they come back?" asked Josh.

"They will be back. The river won't slow them down for long."

"But there might be fifty of them, and there's only one of us," said Will.

"I know. We didn't divert them for long. They've come to attack my village. We need to warn them," said Hawk.

The boys pulled their canoe onto the shore, hid it behind a clump of wild roses, and ran along a little-used path in the woods, back toward Hawk's village. When they were almost there, they left the path and followed the shoreline. By the time they reached the outskirts of the camp, all three of them were out of breath. The sun had flooded the morning sky with light, and the campfires were burning low as the unsuspecting villagers continued to sleep. Hawk grunted as he stepped on a sharp stone, but he ignored the pain and the blood dripping from his foot as he ran into the village. "Wake up! The Dakota are coming!" he shouted.

The men burst out of their wigwams and ran over to him. "What's going on?" asked one of village elders.

"A war party of Dakota is coming. After my father made the truce, they attacked us at our night camp. We escaped, but some of their canoes caught up with us. They followed us down the rapids and they'll be here soon."

The village was instantly filled with commotion. A wrinkled elder barked out a series of commands. Cries of "*Ahgoing-ug!*" passed through the people. Within minutes weapons were loaded into the canoes and the people were lined up in a rough row longer than Josh could see. The elder split them into three divisions. The first group, including Josh and Hawk, set out to look for more Dakota on the water. The second group, including Will and Ellen, stayed back to defend the village. A third group crept through the woods along the river, getting into position so they could capture the Dakota the boys waylaid.

The warmth of the sun caused the mist on the lake to break up, making it easier for the Ojibwa canoes to navigate as they searched for more Dakota. Josh sat with Hawk in the middle of a ten-person canoe. He leaned over the side. "How deep is it here?"

"Why do you want to know?" asked Hawk.

"In case I fall out."

"It's so deep that if you sank to the bottom, we'd never find you. Be quiet. You're supposed to be thinking."

"What am I supposed to be thinking about?"

"The different things that might happen when we meet up with the Dakota and how you're going to handle them. We've already talked about this. Imagine every possible situation and come up with a plan of how you would handle it. You need to be mentally prepared," reminded Hawk, sounding exasperated.

Josh didn't reply. He was too busy looking off into the distance. A group of Dakota canoes had just emerged from around a small island in front of them. They glided to a stop as their surprised warriors tried to figure out what was going on. After a brief pause the Dakota let out a loud war whoop and raced toward the five Ojibwa canoes.

"What's going on?" asked Josh.

"We're going to war. Grab a weapon," replied Hawk.

The wind picked up as the two groups paddled toward one another. They were barely thirty canoe lengths apart when one of the Dakota let out a war whistle and the first volley of arrows flew through the air. Josh ducked as an arrow flew past his head and struck the inside of his canoe.

The Dakota's shrieking and yelling grew more feverish. They hooted and hollered and shook their fists in the air. Their bloodthirsty cries made Josh shudder. "What are we supposed to do?" he whimpered.

Hawk handed him a tomahawk with a wooden handle and a blade made of stone. Another arrow whizzed through the air, landing next to his knee. Five Dakota canoes separated from the pack and paddled toward them, moving into position. The rest of the Dakota canoes went after the others.

"Oh, no! We're surrounded!" he shouted.

TEN

BATTLE OF THE CANOES

The head Dakota canoe charged. The sound of cracking wood and tearing birch bark filled the air as it rammed into Josh and Hawk's canoe. Their canoe emerged a little dented, but still intact, better than their enemy's. The Dakota canoe was no match for them. Even though both vessels were made of birch bark, the Dakota canoe was designed to be light, so it could be carried over a man's head on long portages. It wasn't made for warfare.

The two Dakota began to panic as water poured through the large gap in their canoe. The Ojibwa sat in their strong, heavy canoes, coldly watching their enemy struggle. Finally, the man sitting beside Josh leaned over the side of their canoe and struck the two Dakota with his war club. They fell out of their half-filled canoe, slid under the water, and floated away.

"We got them!" shouted Hawk.

Josh shook his head. "You're crazy."

"Get your tomahawk ready."

The other four Dakota canoes moved in closer. "Get them!" commanded one of the warriors in Josh's boat. When a Dakota canoe pulled

alongside, Josh leaned over and smashed a big hole in it with his tomahawk. The Dakota tried to grab his arm to stop him, but the Ojibwa
protected him. Water quickly flooded the second Dakota canoe, and it
sank below the surface of the water, weapons and all. Hawk managed to
club both Dakotan passengers on the head, causing them to fall face
first into the water.

"This tomahawk works pretty good," said Josh through a painful
grimace, "but I don't like using it."

"You have to keep at it. We're not finished yet. If we don't get
them, they'll get us," said Hawk.

The remaining three Dakota canoes moved in for the kill. They
surrounded Josh's canoe; the only direction they could move was backward, toward the other Ojibwa. "What do we do?" he shrieked.

"We fight. Swamp their canoe," shouted one of the men.

Josh turned to the left. As his fellow warriors fought the two
Dakota with their paddles and clubs, Josh lifted his tomahawk and
smashed the inside of their canoe. The birch bark ripped like a sheet of
paper and water poured in. The two remaining canoes moved closer.
Josh's canoe went after them. With a few more thrusts of his tomahawk,
he destroyed their canoes, too.

Seconds later they were floating alongside some terrified Dakota
thrashing about in the water. They looked up at the Ojibwa, their eyes
unable to hide their fear. Two of them took huge, gasping breaths of air
and disappeared below the surface of the water.

As Josh sat there watching, he felt the canoe wriggle beneath him.
"Um, Hawk …" Before he could finish his sentence, two men from his
canoe stood up and dove into the water. The canoe rocked from side to
side. Josh held on; he thought they might tip. "Good thing Will's not
in here," he muttered as he tried to use his weight to stabilize it.

The Ojibwa swimmers resurfaced a minute later, sucked in a deep
breath of air, and dove back down. "What are they doing?" he asked.

"Getting those two Dakota before they put a hole through our floor with their knives," answered Hawk.

"What?" Josh couldn't help lifting his feet. He scanned the bottom of the canoe. "Where are they?"

One of the Dakota popped out of the water, grabbed the side of the canoe, and tried to hoist himself in. Hawk tried to peel off his fingers. "Josh, help me," he cried.

Josh smashed the blunt end of his tomahawk against one of the man's hands. The warrior grunted in pain and slipped into the water.

"Good job!" cheered Hawk.

There was no time to celebrate. The Ojibwa warriors from Josh's canoe resurfaced, gasping for air. They held up a Dakota warrior between them, like a big fish, and dragged him over to his half-submerged canoe, leaving him to be rescued by his fellow warriors.

Every time Josh thought they were finished, more Dakota canoes came after them. The battle continued for over an hour. One by one, the Ojibwa either overturned or sank the Dakota canoes, until there were only ten left.

Josh looked around; he was relieved to see that all five of their canoes were still intact. The heavy construction gave the Ojibwa the security they needed to attack the Dakota, rather than being forced to simply defend themselves.

As he sat there, a lone Dakota canoe silently paddled up behind them. Josh jerked to one side when he realized a Dakota warrior was near him, glaring angrily. His fellow warriors quickly regrouped while he fumbled for his tomahawk. They began pounding on the Dakota canoe with their clubs. Just when it looked like victory was in sight, one of the Dakota warriors reached in, grabbed Josh by the arm, and pulled him toward their canoe.

"Help! Let me go! Don't let him take me," he screamed. Hawk grabbed him by the ankles and pulled. Josh hung between the two canoes, his body dangling above the water.

The Dakota warrior tugged harder until all of Josh's body but his legs were in his canoe.

Josh's cries grew more feverish. "Hawk, help! Save me!"

Hawk and one of the Ojibwa tried to pull Josh back into their canoe, but all they managed to do was to pull the two canoes closer together.

With one enormous tug, the Dakota captured Josh and quickly paddled off. The Ojibwa canoe sped across the water after them.

Josh tried to jump out, but one of the Dakota warriors pinned him down. "Let me go!" he hollered.

The warrior shook his head. "You destroyed our canoes. You're staying with me."

"No, I'm not," said Josh defiantly. He stood up, ready to escape. The warrior smacked him on the back with his paddle. He sank to his seat in pain. "Hawk, help!" he shouted.

Hawk's canoe plowed through the water after him, but it was bigger and heavier and had a hard time keeping up. Slowly but surely the distance between the two canoes increased. Josh felt a burning sensation flare up in his stomach. *Oh, God, please help me. Please save me from these guys. Don't let me die.*

As they continued across the lake, Josh noticed that some of the islands looked familiar. On his left, he spotted the island where they had camped the night before. The two logs still floated in the water near the beach, and the remains of their campfire were barely visible. *I wonder what happened to everybody. God, please be with them wherever they are.*

As they passed the island, Josh spotted a strange ripple in the water ahead. The warriors in his canoe were so busy trying to escape they didn't notice.

As they neared the ripple, fear gripped Josh's heart; he'd seen a ripple like that before. He pulled his knees to his chest. As he stared at the water, a little stream of bubbles broke through its surface. The warriors in his canoe finally noticed something was amiss and slowed down, trying to figure out what was going on. One of them mumbled something and shrugged his shoulders.

I guess it's nothing, thought Josh.

They were gliding over the spot when two men popped out of the water, grabbed the side of the Dakota canoe, and tipped it over.

Josh screamed as he plunged into the water. He resurfaced seconds later, coughing and sputtering, and swam to the overturned canoe. When he turned to see what was happening, he spotted Great Eagle. He had one of the Dakota in a headlock and was holding him underwater. The man thrashed violently, but he couldn't escape the chief's grasp. His movements gradually slowed and then stopped as he lost consciousness. Great Eagle released him and swam over to help his friend who was battling the other Dakota. When that Dakota saw Great Eagle coming, he gave up and swam away. It would take him a long time to reach the nearest shore.

Just then Hawk's canoe caught up with all of them. "Father!" Hawk shouted. He leaped out of his canoe and swam to his dad. The two of them embraced before climbing back into the Ojibwa canoe. Great Eagle sat on the floor, his weapons still tied to his back. Hawk huddled beside him.

"Father, how did you get here?" he asked.

"It took us a long time to stop those young braves who swam to the island behind the logs. By the time we got them, they had killed or injured half our men and destroyed our canoes. Our only hope was to swim for the village, so I lashed my weapons onto my back and set out to get help. The others are waiting back on the island. What I am more curious about is how the two of you got here."

"While you were busy fighting those Dakota, Josh and Will and I escaped in one of our canoes. On the way back to the village, we ran into a Dakota war party on the lake. It was so foggy that we almost crashed into them. They chased us, but we managed to escape by going down the rapids—"

"—You should have seen us go flying over the waterfall," interrupted Josh.

Hawk smiled. "We hid our canoe in the eddy before the Gap and ran back to the village. One of the elders sent a group of us out to meet the Dakota. The others stayed back."

"And then you saved me," added Josh. "I don't want to think about what they were going to do to me. All I know is it wouldn't have been good. I owe you one."

"You don't owe me anything, son. It is something any brave would have done."

"Thanks," said Josh, his eyes gleaming with unshed tears. "There's just one thing that's bothering me: Why did we have to kill them?"

"We need to teach them that they cannot take advantage of our people. I believe that we should always seek peace before harm, but when the Dakota attack us for no reason, they leave us no choice but to defend ourselves. If we didn't fight back, they would slaughter every one of us—other tribes have suffered this fate. War is terrible for everyone. Now that they know we are a formidable adversary, it is my hope that they will run away like a dog with its tail between its legs and leave us alone for many seasons to come."

By now, the other Ojibwa canoes had joined them. Great Eagle looked at his fellow warriors. "We must return to the village. Our people need our help." Everyone nodded in agreement, and they pointed their canoes toward home.

ELEVEN

DEADFALLS AND SNARES

The prow of Josh's canoe struck the beach, leaving a groove in the wet sand. Josh, Hawk, Great Eagle, and the rest of their crew cautiously crept up the path that led to the camp.

All was quiet at the village; there was no one in sight. The wigwam doors gently flapped in the breeze and the campfires had burned to ashes. It looked like everyone had suddenly vanished.

"Where is everyone?" asked Josh. "There should be a whole bunch of people here."

"Maybe they're hiding in the woods," suggested Hawk.

"What are we supposed to do?"

"We need to find them. Be careful. There might be Dakota around."

Josh trailed behind Great Eagle and the other warriors as they looked inside several of the wigwams. They didn't find anyone. "Spread out," ordered Great Eagle. "We must find our people."

Josh and Hawk crept to the outer edge of the village. "Let's go down there," said Josh, pointing to a narrow path that meandered off into the bush.

He slowly walked down the path, watching for footprints or other signs of recent visitors, but didn't see anything suspicious. Josh turned to Hawk. "How far should we go?"

"A little further," whispered Hawk.

The boys walked on for another minute. Suddenly Josh jerked to a stop. Hawk wasn't expecting this. He crashed into Josh's back. "What are you doing?" he growled.

Josh was so distracted by the pair of beaded moccasins lying in the middle of the path that he didn't answer. He took three more steps, so focused on the moccasins that he didn't notice the brown rope stretched across the path at ankle-height. As his foot connected with the rope, he lost his balance and fell forward.

Josh lay on the ground, dazed. When he got his bearings, he slowly got up. "What's going on? Is somebody trying to kill me?"

Hawk shook his head, trying not to smile. "I'd say somebody was getting ready for the Dakota. The rope was supposed to trip them, not you."

Josh frowned. "But it didn't get them. It got me."

"You need to pay attention to where you're going." Hawk carefully stepped over the rope and continued down the path.

Josh bent down and rubbed his leg. "Thanks for the sympathy."

Finding nothing, the boys doubled back to the village. It was still deserted. Even Great Eagle and the other warriors had vanished. Josh followed Hawk down a different path. They were near the edge of the woods when Josh spotted another rope. This one was strung in a circle between two trees. A piece of deer jerky hung from a tree branch just past it. If Josh stretched his arm through the loop, he would almost be able to reach it.

"I'm not making the same mistake again," he muttered to himself. "I'm not going anywhere near that jerky." He pushed his way past Hawk and carefully stepped through the loop. His left ankle accidentally brushed against the rope, and before he realized what was happening, he felt it tighten around his leg. The thick sapling that was bent over the path twitched, and the rope holding it down released.

A second later, Josh was hanging upside down, suspended in the air.

"Help! I'm trapped!" he shouted.

Hawk stood there, not believing his eyes. "Shhh! I warned you to be careful."

"I didn't know this was a trap. Get me down!"

"Okay, but from now on pay attention to where you're going, and be quiet!"

Hawk grabbed Josh by the chest, pulled him to the ground, and loosened the noose around his leg. Josh slid his ankle out and watched as Hawk reset the trap.

When he was finished, Hawk straightened up and paused for a moment, listening. "I think I heard something. We'd better hide. Follow me." He and Josh ran back to the village and scrambled up a pine tree.

Josh's heart filled with dread when a party of bloodthirsty Dakota emerged over the rocky ridge at the side of the camp. They wore feathered headdresses, and their faces were covered in black and red war paint. They let out a fear-striking war whoop and tore through the camp, surrounding the wigwams. Their leader let out a loud whistle, and they shot volley after volley of arrows into the wigwams, pausing only long enough to reload their bows. When their leader whistled again, they stopped and peered inside. Shouts of rage filled the air when they realized that every single wigwam was empty.

Josh and Hawk watched them regroup. Their leader shouted out more instructions, and they filtered through the camp, looking behind every large rock and tree. Once they realized everyone was gone, their leader gestured toward the paths that radiated out from the camp. An old, wrinkled warrior in their party replied by scrunching up his face and shaking his head. The leader glared at the elder, stamped his feet, and called out more orders. They grabbed their weapons—bows and arrows, spears, thick wooden clubs, and a few knives—broke into smaller groups, and disappeared into the woods.

Hawk looked at Josh and raised his finger to his lips.

Don't worry. I'll sit perfectly still, even if it kills me. The last thing I need is for a pinecone to fall, he thought, remembering his horrible experience in the woods in England.

The boys sat there, as still as statues, as a group of Dakota walked beneath them. Even though they were well hidden by the thick pine boughs, Josh felt a pang of fear in his heart. *I wonder where Will and Ellen are. I hope they're okay. God, please be with them.*

When the Dakota were out of earshot, the boys scrambled down the tree. "What do we do now?" asked Josh.

"Grab some weapons and follow them," ordered Hawk.

"Didn't your people take all the weapons?"

"My father always keeps some extra knives hidden in our wigwam."

"Is it safe to go there?"

"I think so."

"You go; I'll wait here," said Josh.

Hawk disappeared into the village. Josh waited at the side of the path, ready to quickly duck into the bush if anyone came along. As he stood there, he heard the trill of a bird from deep within the forest. He stood a little taller and looked around but couldn't see it. The trill repeated, and then its seven notes were duplicated a tone lower. *That sounds familiar.* Josh wracked his brain, trying to figure out where he had heard that tune before. Suddenly his eyes sparkled and a big smile crossed his face. It was the first seven notes of *Twinkle, Twinkle, Little Star.*

Hawk reappeared behind Josh and touched him on the shoulder. Josh jumped back. "Don't scare me like that," he hissed.

"Sorry."

"My brother is somewhere in the woods; I just heard him whistle. Can we go find him?"

"Are you sure?"

"Positive. He whistled a song he used to play on his violin when he was little. See … there it is again."

Hawk stood there, motionless, as he tried to figure out what direction Will's song was coming from. "He's down the next path. Can you get there without setting off any more traps?"

"You lead. I'll follow," said Josh

Hawk turned and advanced through the woods. No matter how hard Josh tried, he couldn't walk as quietly as his friend. The leaves crunched under his feet, and the rotten logs cracked as the wood split from the pressure of his weight.

Within minutes they reached the other path. There was still no sign of the Dakota. Josh heard his brother's whistle once more; it was very close. Hawk stopped beside a large birch tree. He looked up and pointed. There, high up in the tree, were Ellen and Little Bee, their faces covered in war paint. They held one end of a huge woven net. Will was perched in a tree on the other side of the path, gripping his end of the net with great concentration. He had war paint on, too, but he had botched his job and ended up looking more like someone with a bad case of the measles than a ferocious warrior. The three of them waved madly for Josh and Hawk to get out of the way.

The sound of voices and the thud of footsteps broke the silence. "They're coming," whispered Hawk. "Follow me."

The boys disappeared into the bush in the nick of time. A group of Dakota surged past them and disappeared down the trail.

"Why didn't they drop the net?" whispered Josh.

Hawk shrugged.

Josh looked up at Ellen.

She put her finger to her lips.

He squinted at her, feeling confused, but she didn't respond. She had turned away and was busy watching something out of his sight. He moved off the path.

A bloodcurdling scream echoed through the woods. Josh and Hawk ducked back into the bush and watched as an Ojibwa woman came hurtling toward them, followed by the Dakota. In his excitement, one of the Dakota in the middle of the group forgot to look where he was going. He hit a braided rawhide rope strung across the path and a log hanging overhead came crashing down, knocking him and the other warriors in his group over like a row of dominoes. The two warriors behind them came to an abrupt stop and were watching their trapped comrades when a volley of arrows came flying at them, wounding them instantly.

A loud cry came from further up the path. Josh heard Ellen, Will, and Little Bee cheering. He jumped out from his hiding spot and ran over to see them. Five Dakota were lying on the ground, struggling to escape from under their net. Once they realized they were trapped and outnumbered, they stopped straining and lay there, waiting to see what would happen next.

"Is that all of them?" asked Josh.

Hawk let out a loud whoop in reply. It was answered by a series of shouts from the village. "It sounds like my father just caught the rest of them."

"Already?" said Ellen.

"They're the intruders. They don't know their way around like we do. When we're prepared, it doesn't take us long to stop them."

Josh, Will, Ellen, Hawk, and Little Bee darted up the path. They found Great Eagle and his warriors standing in a circle at the edge of the village, surrounding the rest of the Dakota. They watched as the Ojibwa tied the Dakota's wrists and ankles together and carried them to the canoes. Once their prisoners were loaded, they set out across the water with two other canoes as escorts.

"Where are they taking them?" asked Will.

"To an island at the other end of the lake. They'll leave them there. It will take them the rest of the season to build another canoe. By the time they are able to get off the island, the rest of their people will have moved on to their winter hunting grounds," said Hawk.

"What if they decide to come back and hurt you?"

"We totally humiliated them. They won't be back."

Will turned to his brother. "Did you like our traps?"

"They were awesome. They worked just like the ones we saw on TV last week."

"I know. That's where I got the idea."

"You made them?" gasped Josh.

Will smiled. "It was my idea."

"He did a great job," added Ellen.

"I don't believe it. I'm never going to hear the end of this—my wimpy brother brought down a bunch of Dakota," grumbled Josh.

"What did you do?" asked Ellen.

"I poked a few holes in some birch bark—it was no big deal."

Once the furor had died down, the kids had debriefed with Great Eagle, and the traps were dismantled, Hawk led Josh, Will, and Ellen to a shallow cove. Everyone dove into the water for a swim.

The water was perfectly clear and warm from the heat of the afternoon sun. Josh took a deep breath and floated facedown. He watched the minnows and crayfish scurry about in the sand and rocks beneath him. Then he slowly rolled onto his back and took a deep breath. He could feel the fear and tension of the past few days seep out of his body. As he floated in the gentle waves, a sense of peace washed over him. *Thanks for protecting us, God, and thanks for healing Hawk. I still can't believe you did that!*

He allowed his feet to sink down and began treading water. Will and Ellen looked at him expectantly. He gave them a big smile. "I think life should always be like this."

"What do you mean?" asked Ellen.

"It's so perfect—like when we got here. Everything is so good. The fighting's over, and Hawk is just fine. I don't think it could be any better than this."

"You're right. This does seem like paradise," sighed Ellen.

"Remember what it was like when we got here? We fished and swam and jumped off that cliff—even Will did that—and then everything changed. Hawk was attacked by that cougar, we had to fight the Dakota, we couldn't catch any fish, and we argued all the time. I'm glad we're back at the first way again."

"I wonder why we were sent here?" asked Ellen.

"I think we came so Hawk's people could learn about God," said Will.

"Actually, I've learned a lot about God from them," said Josh. "Have you noticed how they pray about everything? They even pray when they kill an animal. Even though their god is different than ours, they sure are devoted to him. We could learn a few things about how to live from them."

Hawk made his way back to the shore and attached a sharp piece of bone to his fishing line. He added a strip of meat for bait, cast out his line, and pulled in a beautiful walleye. Josh swam over to admire his catch.

"The fish are swimming high today, just like I thought. If there's one, there's bound to be more." Hawk repeated the process until his basket was filled to the brim.

Will and Ellen unfurled their net in the water. They waited for a minute. Ellen was just about to pull her end in when Will stopped her. "Just a minute. I have a feeling about this."

"Oh, not again," groaned Josh.

They waited for another minute.

As Will and Ellen lifted their net out of the water, fish fell out on all four sides. The net bulged precariously as they carried it to shore. They placed it on the ground, well away from the edge of the water, and counted thirty shiny, squirming fish. Will was so excited that he punched his fist into the air and shouted, "Yes!"

"Come on, guys," said Hawk. "Let's head back. It's time for supper."

— TWELVE —

THE FEAST

S omething seems different," observed Josh as the kids
trooped through the village.

"I know what you mean. Everyone seems happier," agreed Ellen.

The women of the village bustled about. Some carried birch-bark
containers of wild rice and berries. Others crouched over hot stones,
cooking long strips of meat. Hawk walked over to the fire by the main
wigwam. A group of women sat around it roasting an animal on a stick,
slowly turning it so it would cook evenly.

Hawk gave the kids a big smile. "We're having a feast—that's why
everyone's in such a good mood."

"What are they roasting? It smells great," said Josh.

"We always eat dog on feast days."

Josh's jaw dropped. "You what?"

Hawk sighed. "Why do you ask so many questions?"

"Are you really cooking a dog?" asked Will.

Hawk rolled his eyes. "That's what I said. There's been a stray
hanging around. That's probably it," said Hawk, pointing to the fire.

Ellen turned away, holding her hand over her mouth so she
wouldn't throw up.

"What's wrong with your sister?" asked Hawk.

"She loves dogs and she's a vegetarian. She wouldn't eat roast dog,"
muttered Josh. "I'm not sure I want to either."

Great Eagle intercepted them as they made their way over to Hawk's mother with their fish. "Come with me," he called out. "The elders wish to speak with you."

Josh turned to his brother. "We just talked with them. Why do they want to see us now? Did we do something wrong?"

"Maybe we're in trouble," whispered Will. "Does anyone have the time stone?"

Josh and Ellen both shook their heads. "They probably just want to talk. Don't worry," soothed Ellen.

The village elders had assembled in a circle near the main wigwam, like at the earlier meeting with the talking stick. Great Eagle motioned for the kids to sit down. They sat in front of him, cross-legged.

There was a long silence. Josh could feel his heart pounding in his chest. It took every ounce of his willpower to keep from fidgeting.

Great Eagle gave him a kindly smile. "My son was almost killed by a cougar the other day. Your God saved him."

Josh nodded in agreement.

"You told us that your God expects you to worship him, not the world that he created."

Josh nodded again.

"And your sister said that your God is invisible."

"That's right," said Ellen. "We can't see him, but we know he's with us."

"Yesterday you told us some words about your God. Tell us them again."

"Jesus, God's Son said, 'I am the way and the truth and the life. No one comes to the Father except through me.'" She gave Great Eagle a cautious smile.

Great Eagle stared at her for a long time. Eventually he raised his hands in the air and closed his eyes. "Oh, Great Spirit of the paleface," he intoned, "we seek your power in our lives. We turn away from the spirits we have been worshiping and turn to you. Please be with us and allow us to worship you."

Ellen opened her eyes and turned to her brothers. "I don't believe it—Great Eagle just became a Christian. That's amazing!"

There was another long silence, and then Great Eagle gave Ellen a contented smile. "Thank you," he said. "You may go now."

Hawk jumped up and sniffed the air. "Come on, guys, it's time to eat!"

Hawk's people gathered around the main campfire to enjoy the outdoor feast. Besides the roast dog flavored with maple syrup, the women had cooked a dish of wild rice with chunks of deer jerky, corn on the cob, carrots flavored with maple syrup, and fresh bannock.

The kids had finished eating and were talking about going on another canoe ride when Great Eagle stood up and clapped loudly until he had everyone's attention.

"My people, these last few days have been difficult. We defended our village against the Dakota, and my son was delivered from the power of death. Both of these victories were ours because of the work of the three paleface children and their God."

Josh felt the heat rise in his cheeks.

"To show our gratitude, I would like to present a headdress to each of them and give them new names, in keeping with their contributions to our people."

Hawk's grandfather came up behind Great Eagle carrying three feathered headdresses. The chief looked expectantly at Josh.

Hawk nudged him with his elbow. "Stand up. He wants to give them to you."

The three of them self-consciously walked over to Great Eagle. The chief gently pulled Ellen to his side.

"Your wise teaching reminds me of the owl. He is able to see things that others cannot. Like the owl, you were able to see through the darkness and show us the light. You courageously shared the truth even though you didn't know how we would respond. For this reason, I present you with this headdress," he said, tenderly placing it on her head, "and we give you a new name: 'Golden Owl.' May you continue to fly on the wings of truth and wisdom."

Ellen looked up and smiled. "Thank you," she sniffled.

Great Eagle walked over to Will. "Your time with us has brought out the eagle in your character. You have sought your best self, the part of your character that soars on the wind, as you learned to fish, dive, and trap. Learn from the eagle—as he flies in great circles in the sky, he observes the world. If you do the same, when you act, you can do so with great understanding. For this reason we name you 'Soaring Eagle.'"

Will stood up as tall as he could and stuck out his chest as Great Eagle placed the last eagle headdress on his head. He gave Great Eagle a grateful smile. "Thank you, sir." He looked as if he would burst with pride.

Finally Great Eagle turned to Josh. "And last, our dear friend, Josh. My first instinct was to name you after the hawk, not only for your friendship with my son, but because your hunting skills and bravery remind me of those of the hawk. After much thought, I have found a better name for you. Your nimble climbing ability and the skill with which you wielded your tomahawk make the choice obvious. From this day forward, we shall call you 'Little Woodpecker.'"

Josh bit his lip, trying to hold back his disappointment. Great Eagle put the last eagle headdress on his head. Everyone cheered and smiled at the three of them. When the chief wasn't looking, Josh looked over to Will and Ellen.

"I don't want to be called 'Little Woodpecker.' I want a good name, something to do with a bear or eagle—you know, a powerful animal. Even a deer would be better than 'Little Woodpecker.'"

"Don't argue. The chief has spoken," taunted Will.

Josh, Will, Hawk, and Ellen hopped into a canoe and began to paddle across the lake. Hawk had put his eagle headdress on, too. The four of them were a regal sight.

"Where are we going?" asked Josh.

"I thought we'd go back to the rock where I first found you," said Hawk.

They passed by a loon with two chicks riding on her back and a flock of clumsy pelicans. Josh smiled as he looked out at the woods and rocks on either side of them. When they reached their destination, Hawk led them up to the rock face. They carefully crept across the ledge, not stopping until they reached the pictures on the rocks.

"Oh, I remember this one," said Will, pointing at the picture of a man joined to a bird by a squiggly line. "What does that mean?"

"That's a medicine man. The bird symbolizes his medicine bag. That's where he gets his power."

"What about that one?" asked Ellen, pointing to the drawing of two people standing side by side. A squiggly line joined the mouth of the smaller person to the hole in the chest of the larger one.

"The tall person is the medicine man. He's giving instructions to a boy."

"What kind of instructions?" asked Josh.

"How to talk with the spirits."

"Can I draw a picture on the rock?" asked Ellen.

"Sure." Hawk opened his hunting bag and took out a bundle of leaves. He carefully unfurled them, revealing a reddish, oily lump inside.

Josh leaned over to take a closer look. "What's that?"

"Rock paint. My grandmother made it."

"What's it made of?"

"A bunch of stuff: berry juice, spruce gum, fish oil, and crushed rock."

Ellen dipped her finger in the paint and moved along the ledge until she found a blank spot on the rocks. Using her finger as a paintbrush, she drew a cloud with a stick person below. In between the two, she added a cross and connected all three with a squiggly line of her own.

Hawk looked puzzled as he tried to interpret her drawing. "What does that mean?"

"That's your father," said Ellen, pointing at her stick person, "and God is up in that cloud. He teaches us about himself through his Son, Jesus. Jesus connects us to God. He sacrificed his life for us on the cross."

"How am I supposed to know all this?" asked Hawk.

"You already know a lot of it. I've watched you pray throughout the day. The only problem is that you were praying to the wrong god. You need to join your father and follow God and Jesus instead of worshiping creation."

"I think I've seen your Jesus."

"What?" exclaimed Ellen. "When?"

"During my vision quest. Most of my people have animals come and teach them in their dreams, but a man came to me."

"What did he look like?"

"I don't know; he's kind of hard to describe. He looked a lot like my people, and he had the kindest eyes I'd ever seen. He told me about the cross."

"No way! God must have been preparing you for our visit. What else did he tell you?"

"He said that I should turn away from worshiping animals and look to him for everything I need, because he would always be with me and take care of me."

"Why didn't you tell us this before?" asked Josh.

"I didn't know what it meant. It was so different than what everyone else experiences during their vision quests."

"So God's been teaching you, even though you don't have a Bible and you'd never heard about Jesus. That's amazing!" said Josh.

"You're going to do just fine," added Ellen.

Will glanced down at the ground and spotted a fist-sized stone. He picked it up, let out a shout of joy, and began jumping up and down. "It's the time stone! I found the time stone!"

"Already?" lamented Josh.

"Yes, already! It's time to go home."

As the four of them stood there, a smattering of clouds passed overhead, sprinkling them with warm, misty rain. Josh was thinking about the events of the past few days when a magnificent rainbow appeared in the sky.

"Look," exclaimed Ellen. She beamed at Hawk. "I can see both ends of it. Isn't it beautiful?"

He stood there, not saying a word.

The rainbow was just starting to fade when an eagle soared overhead, appearing to touch the clouds as it glided on the thermal currents. Hawk bowed his head as if to pray.

Ellen gently touched him on the shoulder. "You're not praying to the eagle, are you?"

"No. I'm thanking my new God for the beautiful world he made and for the eagle."

"Whew," said Josh, running the back of his hand across his forehead. "You had me scared for a minute."

"Do you know what I like about the eagle?" asked Ellen.

Hawk looked at her expectantly.

"It reminds me of what life is like when you trust God. You can fly through life with confidence, knowing that God is the wind beneath your wings. You don't always know where He will take you, but you know He will always be with you. We can rest in Him."

Suddenly everything grew dark, and the rocks around them started to quiver. The three of them grabbed on to each other. Hawk quickly backed away.

When Josh, Will, and Ellen opened their eyes, they were back home, sprawled out among the rows of vegetables in their garden.

Josh let out a big sigh. "We made it. What a great trip. I can hardly wait to go again."

THE END.

So there is a special rest still waiting for the people of God.
For all who enter into God's rest will find rest from
their labors, just as God rested after creating the world.
Let us do our best to enter that place of rest.
Hebrews 4:9–11 (NLT)

TERROR IN HAWK'S VILLAGE

Spiritual Building Block: Worship

THINK ABOUT IT

The fourth commandment teaches us about the Sabbath, a day of rest. It says: "Remember the Sabbath day by keeping it holy. Six days shall you labor and do all your work, but the seventh day is a Sabbath to the LORD your God…" (Exodus 20:8–11).

The Sabbath we are supposed to "remember" started at the time of creation. After God made the world, he rested. God didn't rest because he was tired, but because he was satisfied. Everything he made was good. This didn't mean God stopped doing things, but that the world he created was complete. It was at peace.

Adam, the first man, was able to stay in this glorious place of rest with God until he and Eve sinned by eating the fruit from the forbidden tree in the Garden of Eden. Their sin disturbed the perfect world that God had made for his people.

The world stayed in this sorry state until Jesus came. Jesus' death on the cross changed everything. It brought us back to the "rest" at the time of creation, because he put the world back on track. Now all people can live at peace with God. We don't have to make sacrifices to gain forgiveness because Jesus wiped out all our sin forever.

Many years ago, the rest of the seventh day, which used to take place on Saturday, was moved to Sunday. It became a reminder of

Easter, the day when Jesus triumphed over death and rose from the dead. On Sunday, Christians remember what Jesus did for them through his death on the cross.

Talk About It

When Josh and his siblings first landed near Hawk's village, everything was perfect. Josh felt like he was back at the time of creation, before sin entered the world. Remember how he said his heart was filled with peace?

Then conflict came into the picture. It wasn't serious at first: the kids started to fight, the fishing didn't go as well, and Little Bee began to drive Josh crazy. In a very short time, the conflict grew. A wild cougar turned on Hawk. The Dakota attacked, made a truce, and attacked again. Just about everything possible went wrong. When the fighting finally stopped, Hawk's world went back to the way it was at the beginning. Everything was right again, and Josh rediscovered that same sense of peace. His experiences in Hawk's village are similar to the ones that people have had throughout the history of the world when they became Christians. The conflict in their lives—the sin, the fighting, the unhappiness—was replaced with peace.

What does remembering the Sabbath (or Sunday) mean for us today? Think of it as a sign. Just as God put a rainbow in the sky to remind us that he would never flood the earth again, the Sabbath is a sign of the wonderful life we have with Jesus. It is a day where we can slow down, spend time remembering what God has done for us, and worship him.

Remembering the Sabbath isn't about keeping a list of rules, like not mowing your lawn or not reading any books except for the Bible on that day. God didn't have a list of do's and don'ts in mind when he gave us this commandment. Rather, he saw that we needed a day to slow down and remember him.

The Ten Commandments are not laws of the land, like speed limits or other laws we're not supposed to break. They are more like the loving instruction a father and mother gives to their children, so they will learn the way to live that is best for them.

The important thing to remember is that whatever you choose to do, take time every Sunday to think about God and Jesus and remember the wonderful things they have done in your life. Think about how you can live your life in a way that tells others that you believe God is holy.

TRY IT

When we accept Jesus as our Savior, we have new life in him. This doesn't mean that every part of our lives will be instantly perfect, but that we can always turn to Jesus for help, no matter what kind of trouble we find ourselves in. He loves to show us the best way to live. The Bible is full of Jesus' teachings. It has given people guidance for thousands of years.

If you haven't accepted Jesus as your Savior, you are missing out on the best life possible. If you say yes to Jesus, you won't always be able to do things your way, but you will discover that living God's way is the best way. Don't be afraid to invite Jesus into your heart.

Next time you're out, take time to notice the signs around you. How many different kinds can you see? What do they tell you? Did you change where you were going or what you were doing because of them?

Think of how you can make Sunday a day that's a special sign of what Jesus is doing in your life.

You might have a favorite song about God that you like to sing. If you sing it to yourself throughout the day, it can remind you of the good things he is doing in your life. Memorize a passage of Scripture that will help you think about God. The Bible is full of good verses to learn. One good one is 1 Thessalonians 5:17. It says, "Be joyful always; pray continually; give thanks in all circumstances, for this is God's will for you in Christ Jesus."

Consider sitting down with a parent, teacher, or a pastor and talk about how you can remember God this Sunday, as well as during the rest of the week.

Use these signs to help you turn the right way when you are tempted to do something you know is wrong.

TREACHERY IN THE ANCIENT LABORATORY

If you thought *Terror in Hawk's Village* was great, wait until you read *Treachery in the Ancient Laboratory*. But you don't have to wait at all—here's a sneak peak at this exciting adventure also releasing September 2004.

• CHAPTER 6 •
DRASTIC MEASURES

Josh propelled his body over the wall and landed in the cemetery. Hundreds of gravestones covered in Hebrew characters were arranged in rows throughout the lush, park-like space. Many of the stones had sunk partly into the ground. Others were tipped at awkward angles. As he meandered around, he had to watch his steps carefully because the ground was so uneven.

"This cemetery was started over one hundred years ago. It's been full a long time, but this is all the space they were given, so they had to start burying people one on top of the other." Ben brushed away a spider web that was strung between two gravestones. "If you look at the stones, they often tell you something about the person buried there." He pointed to one with two hands arranged side by side. "That means a rabbi was buried here. See that one?" He pointed to a pair of scissors. "That person was a tailor."

"Look, a book! Maybe that person was a writer," said Ellen.

"Actually, that stands for a printer. I've seen tweezers for a doctor, a mortar and pestle for an apothecary, and a lute for an instrument maker."

"Then how do you explain this?" asked Josh, pointing to a rose on one of the gravestones.

"Her name was 'Rose,'" said Ben, grinning.

"Oh. I thought maybe she sold flowers."

"What's with the piles of stones everywhere? Don't they ever clean this place up?" asked Will.

"People leave pebbles on the graves as a sign of respect," said Ben.

Josh walked over to a particularly ornate headstone. "Then this guy must have been really important. He's got a huge stone, and look at all those pebbles."

"That's Rabbi Loew's grave. When he died last year, there was a lot of wailing. It carried on for days."

"Why?"

"He's a legend around here, you know, for the *Golem*."

"The what?"

"You've never heard of Rabbi Loew's Golem?"

Josh shook his head.

"The rabbi made a giant man out of clay."

"Big deal. We could do that, too," said Will.

Ben shook his head, barely able to hide his irritation. "I bet you couldn't bring one to life."

"How'd he do that?" asked Josh.

"He made a giant man out of clay, chanted some spells from the Cabala, engraved the word *emet*—that means truth—on his forehead, and the giant came to life."

Josh's eyes lit up. "Wow. Can you get me a book of those spells?"

"No way. The Golem was made for a specific purpose. His job was to stop the people who were spreading lies about the Jews and persecuting them. Trust me, you wouldn't want to mess with the Golem."

"Where is he now?" asked Ellen.

"Eventually the emperor promised to protect the Jews, so Rabbi Loew took the Golem aside and told him they didn't need his help anymore. The Golem didn't like that, so the rabbi quickly erased the first letter from his forehead, changing *emet* to *met*, which means death, and the Golem died. That night, the rabbi and his helpers hauled the Golem's clay into the attic of the synagogue and covered it with old prayer books. They say it's still there."

"Can we go see it? Please, please, please?" begged Josh.

"We're not breaking into the synagogue. That would be a terrible thing to do," said Ben.

"Come on. We wouldn't hurt anything. I just want to take a look."

Will cleared his throat. "Remember what happened the last time you said that?"

"Ben's right. The reason we're in this cemetery is because you used a match to 'take a look,' and look what that got us. Trouble . . . big trouble," said Ellen.

"I'm with Ellen. We're done exploring for today. What do we do now?" asked Will.

"Find a comfortable spot for the night. We'll head back in the morning," said Ben.

"But I don't want to sleep here," said Will.

"Too bad," said Josh. He didn't feel one bit sorry for his brother.

Will sat down, his back to the wall, muttering away as he tried not to notice the way the breeze moved the leaves of the elder trees that shaded the cemetery, or the long, dark shadows the moon created behind each gravestone.

Ellen sat down with Ben, chatting happily.

Josh lay down on the grass on top of one of the higher graves, closed his eyes, and fell asleep.

The sun wasn't quite up when Will woke everyone up.

Josh rolled onto his side. "Where am I?" he muttered. He opened his eyes a crack. "Oh, that's right, the cemetery."

Will nudged him again.

"Leave me alone. I'm still sleeping."

"We need to get out of here. I'm exhausted. I spent the whole night standing guard, just in case the Golem came back to life and decided to get us."

"That's nice," mumbled Josh.

Frustrated by his brother's response, Will walked over to Ellen and Ben, who were already awake.

"Can we go back to Uncle Pepik's now?" asked Ellen.

"We can try. We'll walk to the lane together. You can hide while I see my uncle and make sure everything's okay. If it is, I'll come get you." Ben let out a big yawn. "I'm with Josh. I didn't get enough sleep, either. It's going to be a long day."

The walk back to Golden Lane was uneventful. The streets were quiet, except for the crowing of roosters. Josh pranced over the Charles Bridge, swinging his arms back and forth as though he didn't have a care in the world, while the others trudged along behind.

They sneaked into the castle grounds through Daliborka. The tower was completely empty, so they stopped for a minute to survey the damage done by Josh's gunpowder. The room was intact, but the walls were covered in a layer of black soot.

"Good thing I didn't have more gunpowder, or I'd have blown the place up," said Josh.

"And killed all of us in the process," complained Will.

"Come on, we have to keep moving. We had better be quiet. Most of the alchemists will have been up all night tending their furnaces. I don't want any of them to see us," said Ben.

"Why not?" asked Josh.

"I don't trust the people around here. Everyone is out for themselves. They'll squeal on you in a heartbeat if they think it will keep them on the emperor's good side. We can't afford to take any chances."

They left the tower and walked down Golden Lane. Ben stopped. "Wait over there," he said, pointing to a narrow alleyway. "I'll come get you if everything's all right."

Will wrapped his arms around his chest. "What if you don't come back?"

"Then you're on your own." He slipped away before Will could question him further.

The three of them trudged down the narrow alleyway between the two buildings. Josh looked back over his shoulder. Six of the emperor's guards marched down the lane after Ben. "Oh, no," he exclaimed.

"What?" said Will.

"I just saw six guards go after Ben. I think he's in trouble."

"This is your fault. I'm holding you responsible."

"What do you mean? How can you blame me for this?"

"Number one: You touched the stone after I specifically asked you not to. There might have been a better place for us to go, but you didn't even give us a chance to find out.

Number two: You set Rudolph's tapestry on fire. If you hadn't been so stupid and lit that match, we wouldn't have been sent to Daliborka to be executed."

Will's voice grew frantic as he continued. "Number three: If we hadn't gone to Daliborka, you wouldn't have lit that gunpowder, and we wouldn't have been forced to run away and spend the night in the cemetery, and I would have gotten some sleep. I'm going to have a lousy day, and it's all your fault!"

Josh could feel his temper bubbling up inside of him. He looked around for something to throw, but the only thing in the alleyway was a tiny gray kitten that mewed as it rubbed against Ellen's leg. He glared at his brother for a long minute, and then, just when Will thought everything was going to be okay, Josh wound up and punched him as hard as he could, right in the stomach.

Will bent over, moaning and gasping for air. Ellen rushed to his side to help, but he pushed her away.

"What did you do that for?" asked Ellen, her voice rising. She wiped a tear from her eye. "If Dad were here, he'd ground you for a month, and you know it."

"I'm tired of being picked on all the time. He thinks everything is my fault." Josh's eyes filled with tears. "It's not my fault he's such a wimp. He should learn how to handle things better. I've been doing the best I can. I didn't mean to make so much trouble." He raised his voice and yelled, "And just so you know, I'm tired and hungry, too!"

"I don't care. That's no excuse."

"Fine. Side with him if you want. From now on, I'm on my own." He stalked down the alleyway and turned the corner toward Uncle Pepik's house.

"Ah, Joshua, there you are, and just in time. I need someone to load up the athanor with charcoal. I must say, I prefer charcoal as opposed to that ancient wood-burning furnace I had in my other laboratory," said Uncle Pepik.

"Is it safe for me to be here? Aren't the guards after us?"

"All is well. After several hours of exasperating conversation with the commander, he agreed that the whole situation was a big misunderstanding and decided to set you free. There is one provision, however. I had to promise that I would keep you under my wing and ensure that you didn't get into any more trouble, so no more fires or explosions. You must be on your best behavior, or the commander assured me you'd be left to die in Daliborka."

Josh plopped down on a nearby chair and sat there, hunched over. "I guess that's all right, but it'll cramp my style," he mumbled.

"What was that, son?"

"Oh, nothing. How much charcoal should I put in the fire?"

"More than you put into that black powder you made," replied Uncle Pepik, chuckling. "I still can't believe you blew up my laboratory. My goodness, what a surprise. I now understand what Sir Roger Bacon meant in his Latin anagram of 1242. He was describing how to make the exact mixture you created. I read his instructions many times and never quite grasped them, but now I do. Your little experiment greatly enlightened me. Thank you."

"Um, you're welcome, I think. Where's Ben?"

"He went to get your brother and sister. They'll be back shortly."

"Too bad," muttered Josh, carefully pouring a shovel full of charcoal into Pepik's athanor.

When Ben returned with Will and Ellen, they joined Josh in assisting Pepik. Ellen and Will washed the glass alembics and earthenware containers and arranged them in rows above the workbench, taking care to avoid their brother as much as possible. Josh kept the furnace stoked with charcoal, regularly opening and closing the vents so the temperature remained constant. Uncle Pepik carefully measured different powders, liquids, and dried plants, which he placed in the cucurbit, the lower part of the container that held the materials being distilled. Josh helped him fit the alembic on top, with its long, narrow spout for the condensation to pour out, and they sealed the two pieces together with lute, a sticky mixture made of dung and egg whites.

They were about to break for lunch—scrambled egg yolks, stale bread, and a lump of disgusting cheese—when Scottie and his dogs poked their heads through the door.

"Well, well, Old Pepik, you certainly are full of surprises. Here you are, in a brand new lab that you do not deserve, working with not one, but four assistants. How nice," he snickered.

Pepik looked up from his work. "I'm sorry, but I can't spare the time to visit. I'm at a critical stage in my work. Is there something I can do for you?"

"When I appeared in the emperor's court this morning I was dismayed to learn that you had been granted permission to work with four assistants, when so many of us on Golden Lane have none. When I brought this to the commander's attention, he immediately agreed that an injustice had been done."

Pepik didn't bother to look up from his work. "And your point?"

"In order to rectify this situation, the emperor has proclaimed that there will be a contest tomorrow morning. The first alchemist to produce the philosopher's stone will be awarded these four young people as apprentices, as well as more apparatus, supplies, and a personal servant to cook and clean for them. I suggest you be prepared, old man, because I, Edward Geronimo Scotta, expect to be the victor."

Scottie stared at Pepik, holding his breath as he waited for his reply. Pepik looked at him, closed his eyes, and stood there, gently swaying back and forth.

Scottie finally gave up, turned on his heel, and stomped off, with Apollo and Zeus ambling along behind.

Ben rushed over to his uncle. "Uncle Pepik, what's the matter? Are you okay?"...

What has happened to Uncle Pepik?
And what about Ben?
And is something wrong with Scottie?

Find out what has happened when you read
Treachery in the Ancient Laboratory.

Releasing September 2004.

The Word at Work Around the World

A vital part of Cook Communications Ministries is our international outreach, Cook Communications Ministries International (CCMI). Your purchase of this book, and of other books and Christian-growth products from Cook, enables CCMI to provide Bibles and Christian literature to people in more than 150 languages in 65 countries.

Cook Communications Ministries is a not-for-profit, self-supporting organization. Revenues from sales of our books, Bible curricula, and other church and home products not only fund our U.S. ministry, but also fund our CCMI ministry around the world. One hundred percent of donations to CCMI go to our international literature programs.

CCMI reaches out internationally in three ways:

• Our premier International Christian Publishing Institute (ICPI) trains leaders from nationally led publishing houses around the world.

• We provide literature for pastors, evangelists, and Christian workers in their national language.

• We reach people at risk—refugees, AIDS victims, street children, and famine victims—with God's Word.

Word Power, God's Power

Faith Kidz, RiverOak, Honor, Life Journey, Victor, NexGen — every time you purchase a book produced by Cook Communications Ministries, you not only meet a vital personal need in your life or in the life of someone you love, but you're also a part of ministering to José in Colombia, Humberto in Chile, Gousa in India, or Lidiane in Brazil. You help make it possible for a pastor in China, a child in Peru, or a mother in West Africa to enjoy a life-changing book. And because you helped, children and adults around the world are learning God's Word and walking in his ways.

Thank you for your partnership in helping to disciple the world. May God bless you with the power of his Word in your life.

For more information about our international ministries, visit www.ccmi.org.